COME AS YOU ARE

Praise for Come As You Are

"Ivan's innocent and unwitting flirtation with the demonic is first-rate supernatural horror. Ramirez's characters are beautifully defined, particularly Ivan and Hershey, the school janitor, who turns out to be much more than that. His plot is beautifully scripted and the suspense and supernatural dread emanating throughout this story make it impossible to put down until the last page is read."

— Readers' Favorite

"A chilling YA horror novella. There is no telling what direction this novella is going to swing, as the surprises come quickly. *Come As You Are* is successful at sending chills down your spine over the course of a fast and enjoyable read."

— Self-Publishing Review

"Out of all the elements I liked about the collection, it is the character display that stood out the most. Ramirez truly is a master at bringing his cast to life, and then binding you to their ordeal. Overall, I think it is a stunning collection many readers will enjoy."

— Horror Palace

Books by Steven Ramirez

Jane Doe Cycle

Brandon's Last Words

Faithless

Sarah Greene Mysteries

The Girl in the Mirror

House of the Shrieking Woman

The Blood She Wore

Tell Me When I'm Dead

Tell Me When I'm Dead

Dead Is All You Get

Even The Dead Will Bleed

Other Books

Chainsaw Honeymoon

Come As You Are: A Short Novel and Nine Stories

Come As You Are: A Novella

Glass Highway
Los Angeles, CA
stevenramirez.com

Publisher's Note: This is a work of fiction. Names, characters, places, and incidents are a product of the author's imagination. Locales and public names are sometimes used for atmospheric purposes. Any resemblance to actual people, living or dead, or to businesses, companies, events, institutions, or locales is completely coincidental.

Come As You Are / A Short Novel and Nine Stories / Steven Ramirez. —1st ed.
ISBN-13: 978-0-9990791-1-9

Edited by Shannon A. Thompson
Cover design by Adrijus Guscia

COME AS YOU ARE

and Other Stories

STEVEN RAMIREZ

Glass Highway
LOS ANGELES, CALIFORNIA

For Danielle DeVor, the baddest quiet vampire I know.

No one can tell what goes on in between the person you were and the person you become. No one can chart that blue and lonely section of hell. There are no maps of the change. You just come out the other side.

— Stephen King, *The Stand*

COME AS YOU ARE

Come As You Are

OLLIE WAS THE FIRST. HE WAS MY BEST FRIEND.

My parents don't know—can't know—the whole story, but when it comes right down to it, none of this is even my fault. All I did was read off a bunch of words from a list I found, and the next thing I know, people are dying. Okay, there might have been some supernatural shit involved, but… It's not like I meant for it to happen. I just wanted to keep Kirk Wardell and his loser friends from hurting me again. This was about those assholes, not me. Why did Ollie have to get mixed up in it? It was that damned freakin' list.

This is not my fault.

You always wish you could control who gets what's coming to them, like God. Sort of. But I guess it doesn't work that way. People you never meant to harm—guys like Ollie who were cool to you and bought you a Klondike bar or a Choco Taco because you never had any money in your pocket because your dad's been out of work since forever and your mom's doing all she can to "stretch a dollar"—why did those people have to suffer? It makes no sense.

So I'm sitting in my living room, waiting for the cops to be done talking to Mom and Dad. I should've never said anything. Then my parents wouldn't have called them. Whatever. The detectives will want to ask me what happened at the skate park, and I will lie. Because I may be only twelve, but there's one thing I know: you never tell the truth to the cops. Ever.

I guess I should start at the beginning when things weren't so bad. When Kirk and those doofs he likes to hang out with were making fun of my clothes and my shoes and my hair, and I would just take it like the poor dog next door who keeps getting beaten by Luckman, the mean old neighbor with the missing leg. All the animal does is whimper, lower his head and…take it some more. Yeah, that was pretty much the start of another bitch of a day for me.

ME AND OLLIE had planned to go to Gasher's Park right after school to ride our skateboards. We had to hurry, though, because later the high schoolers would show, and it would be over for us. We'd have to run away before those loudmouthed douches could steal our boards or fling beer bottles at our heads. It could turn into a real mess, let me tell you.

But it was great whenever we got there early. We'd ride and ride for like, maybe half an hour. But then the shit would start. Those dickheads would storm in through the heavy chain link gate, hollering about some little pussies trying to take over their turf. It would always turn into a game of cat and mouse. I guess you know who the mice were. We'd have to try and get past them, through the gate, down the sidewalk, and onto Pear Street.

Usually, we'd make it, but sometimes, they would catch us and throw us up against the fence. One time, Ollie hit his head on a steel post. The blow knocked him out cold, and when he went down, those idiots got scared and took off. Maybe they thought they'd killed him.

"Ollie, jeez!" I said, running up to him and shaking him by the shoulders.

"Are they gone?"

"What? Yeah, they're gone. You mean—"

"I was faking."

Then he sat up, grinning as he wiped the blood off his forehead. I wanted to kill the little turd, but instead, I hugged him.

"Come on, Ollie," I said, giving him my hand.

Anyways, today was pretty much like all the other days, except we left before the shitlickers even arrived. We cut through the park like we always did. Then we decided to sit on a bench next to some old lady who was kissing her pug or whatever.

All of a sudden, Ollie says, "Aww, man! I forgot my math homework."

"You'll get it tomorrow."

"No, Ivan. It's *due* tomorrow. I already got a D in the class, and my dad said if I fail math, he's going to kill me."

"He's not going to kill you, Ollie. It's an exaggeration. Look, you can copy mine."

"You don't understand. Mr. Ryan wrote down special instructions to help me. I need that paper."

Now I'm worried because Ollie is crying like a baby. I mean, big ol' tears that magnify the freckles on his cheeks. I don't know what to say, so I try doing a funny handstand. But I fall on my ass. I'm hoping I can make Ollie laugh.

He isn't even looking at me, though. Now I have a sore ass, and he's still crying.

"Tell you what, Ollie. Let's go back to school and get your math. Come on. I'll walk with you."

"Yeah?" he says. He's smiling, green snot leaking out of his nose, and I know he'll be okay.

We go back the way we came, past the enclosed skate park. The high schoolers we hate are in there, swearing at each other and holding onto beers as they do tricks—backsides, Caballerials, Nollies—stuff me and Ollie are just starting to learn. One of them looks like he's going too fast. He falls and does a wicked face-plant, his beer shattering all over the place.

"Whoa!" someone says. "Dude…"

As we sneak up to the gate, I recognize the kid on the ground. I'm pretty sure his name is Franklin. He's screaming and trying to grab his face, but his friends are holding down his arms. We can see the broken neck of the beer bottle sticking out where his eye should be. I've never seen anything like it in real life—only in horror movies. It looks like the broken bottle gouged out the 'tard's eye. I don't think he even realizes how bad it is. He keeps saying over and over, "I can't see!"

"He's the kid who slammed me into the pole," Ollie says. "Remember?"

When I turn to my friend, he's smiling in a way that is seriously messed up.

———

IT TAKES us only a couple minutes to make it to school. Me and Ollie, we live real close, so it's nice in the morning when we're late and we need to run like hell to be in our seats for English before the tardy bell rings, which only happens, like, five days a week.

As I suspect, the place is pretty much deserted. Janitors are already inside the classrooms, mopping and straightening up and whatnot. We head straight for our lockers. I figure this won't take long. Ollie will find his stupid homework; then we'll go to his house, because there's never any food at my house, and Ollie says there's always too much at his. He'll fix me a burrito, which he likes to call a "bean and cheeser." Later, I'll head home alone, which is no biggie.

Ollie is digging through his locker, looking for the "special" math paper from Mr. Ryan. I'm not doing anything, just chillin'. I look over again. Now, my friend has his stupid head stuck inside his locker. Since he's wasting all my time, I decide to go exploring.

There's this old section of the school that's closed off. Some say it's haunted. As I stare through the chain link fence, I can see the rows and rows of old tan lockers, all of which are closed—except for one. I'd seen this locker before whenever I would pass by in the morning on my way to history. And the only reason I even noticed it at all was because it has this ugly red stain across the door—rust, I think. If you stare at that stain long enough, you begin to see stuff. Not like Jesus or aliens or anything—just weird shapes that kind of move around all swirly.

But, like I said, today the locker is open.

Though no one is supposed to go back there, they never keep the gate locked. I guess it's because most of the other kids are too scared. I'll bet it was the principal who started the "haunted" rumor. But I decide to check it out for shits and giggles, which is what my dad always used to say, back when he had a job. I open the latch and go inside. I can't explain it, but as I move closer to the open locker, a powerful feeling comes over me. Not like fear or anything —more like anticipation. I don't expect to find anything, but as I said, I have nothing else to do, so why the hell not?

The door is swinging back and forth, which is nuts because there isn't even a breeze. To prove to myself I'm not scared, I walk up and shut the door. The stain seems darker—deeper. I look at it all different ways, turning my head this way and that, squinting at it first with my right eye, then with my left. And each time, the shapes look different. If I stare at the door just right, I can almost see...

"What the hell are you doing back here?" someone says.

My heart almost explodes like a water balloon hitting the sidewalk. One of the janitors—this old dude named Hershey—is standing next to me with one hand holding onto his favorite cart with the squeaky wheel from hell. Hershey always smells bad—like sweat and bean farts— and he's missing a lot of teeth. I think he was here when they built the freakin' school. And he's always mad. Maybe his back hurts, which is what my mom always says when some grown-up is being mean to me. *Maybe their back hurts, Ivan. You should feel sorry for them.*

"I'm not doing anything."

He grunts, reaches over, and slams the locker shut. Then he spins the combination lock several times.

"Stay away from here, asswipe. I won't tell you twice."

Hershey turns his cart around and walks toward the gate. As I follow him, I ignore his attitude because I want to find out more about the locker. What's the worst he can do to me anyways? He's a *janitor*.

"Hey, Hershey?"

"Yeah?" he says, a little bit calmer now that he got to yell at a seventh grader.

"Who did that locker belong to?"

"No one."

We're outside the fence now, and he's on his knees, checking the supplies on the cart.

"Well, someone must've used it."

He gets up with a groan and stares at me, his toothless pie-hole hanging open like he can't believe someone has the balls to hit him with all these dumb questions.

"Craig," he says.

"So, is he still a student here?"

"No."

"Oh, he promoted then."

"Sure. He promoted."

The old man shakes his head like some sad, evil clown, which creeps me out the way Ollie did when Franklin lost his eye. I see my friend approaching, grinning and waving his math homework. The two of us are standing next to the gate, staring at the sketchy old man to see what he'll do next. He doesn't disappoint. Rolling his cart straight ahead, one wheel squeaking like a mouse on Spice, he walks like half a mile down, then stops and turns around.

"Be seein' you boys," he says, his raspy voice making this weird echo. "Don't forget what I said. I'll be watching."

After Hershey is gone, I take another look at the locker. Amazingly, it's open again.

"Hey, want to see what's inside that locker over there?"

"I dunno, Ivan," Ollie says. "Let's go."

"Come on, you pussy. Can't you see? Hershey was just messing with us."

"We're not supposed to go back there. Anyway, I needa go home and start on this math."

"Sure you don't want to see what's in Craig's locker?"

"I gotta go. See you tomorrow."

I have no idea what's gotten into my friend, but he

takes off like Sonic, hopping on his skateboard and pushing off down the sidewalk.

"Loser!"

I take a look around to make sure Hershey is gone; then I slip back inside. Taking one more look at the locker door, I decide to open it all the way. It's not even late, but for some reason, the interior of the locker is dark. I can barely make out anything in there. I wait for my eyes to adjust, then reach in toward the back, and I feel the familiar thin, wiry binding of a spiral notebook. Excited, I bring it out into the light. It doesn't look all that weird. It's old and dusty and dog-eared. The cover is flat black, with the words COLLEGE RULED embossed in silver in the lower right-hand corner.

"What's the big deal? Just some stupid notebook."

Bored and a little disappointed, I take a step back and fling it at the locker, trying to make it go inside. But it hits the corner of the opening and lands on the ground, open to the first page. I look down to see what's written there.

Whoever this Craig kid was, he was a pretty good artist. He'd used colored pens to create a title page, which reads, CRAIG'S LIST. The writing reminds me of something I'd seen one time at the public library. There was this traveling exhibit of famous manuscripts and crap, and I remember this style of writing is called calligraphy. That's what the page looks like, only it isn't real calligraphy because Craig hadn't done it with special pens and brushes. Maybe he was like me, and all he could afford were cheap ballpoint pens.

As I pick it up, I notice he had decorated the page with these funny little creatures—kind of like monsters. It looks to me like they're dancing in a big perfect ring surrounding the title. I'm about to turn to the next page when I hear Hershey's squeaky wheel. Before he can round the corner,

I race through the gate, set down my skateboard, tuck the notebook under my arm, and beat it out of there. Easy peasy.

MY SISTER BETH, who's older than me by four years, is home from cheerleading practice. I could never understand it. Beth is as poor as me, but for some reason, she's popular. I guess part of the reason is because Mom taught her how to sew when she was nine. She makes herself all these nice outfits, which are always on fleek. Also, she babysits, which gives her enough money for a cell phone and makeup and stuff.

I don't hate my sister, though it's true she suffers from resting bitch face. And yeah, she always gives me and Ollie a ride to school when it rains. I don't know. It's just that I wish she was more like me, so I could have somebody to talk to besides Ollie. Beth doesn't understand anything about me. Maybe that's the way she likes it. She is so basic.

After a dinner of beans and franks, which my father says is the whole reason air freshener was invented, I head back to my room to do homework. I'm actually a pretty good student, and I don't have to try all that hard. I can usually finish English, math, history, and science in about an hour, give or take. Also, I like to read. I have a strong B average, which is why the principal Mr. Charbonneau put me on the stupid honor roll without my permission.

Mom is always telling me I could be a straight-A student if I wanted to. It wouldn't be difficult. But then they'd stick me in Honors, and I wouldn't be able to see Ollie during the day, except at lunch and PE. And Ollie doesn't have any other friends, even though his parents are well off.

After finishing my history essay, I put everything away in my backpack and bring out the notebook. I make sure my door is locked—which is a joke, really. I mean, it's not like anyone in this family is interested in talking to me. Usually, Dad is out in the garage, working on the car or fixing the lawnmower for, like, the millionth time. And Mom is in the kitchen cleaning up while watching some lame-ass reality show. And Beth. After her homework is done, she spends the rest of the night talking to her dumb friends on her cell phone. So, I'm pretty much alone to do whatever I want.

I'm not sure why, but I keep Craig's notebook hidden under my bed. It's like it's this secret thing I'm not supposed to share with anyone—not even Ollie. I'm lying on my bed now, looking at the first page. Holy crap! I could swear the little monsters Craig had drawn are differ-ent. It's like they've all moved clockwise on the page —*together.* I look at my hand, and it's shaking. I tell myself I'm imagining the whole thing and turn to the next page.

It's a list.

There on the page, printed neatly in large block letters, are five things the reader, I guess, is supposed to do, according to this Craig kid.

1. NEED THE POWER
2. ABSORB THE POWER
3. TEST THE POWER
4. AFFIRM THE POWER
5. SURRENDER TO THE POWER

Staring at that page, I am struggling to understand what the list is even good for. Was this something Craig was telling himself when he wrote it down? I don't know anything about him. Had he been bullied like me? He could've just as well been talking about tae kwon do or karate or some shiz. Or maybe he'd been practicing some kind of New Age mental exercise to make himself feel stronger, so he could make it all the way through middle school without killing himself like Dexter Rodine, who in sixth grade decided to slice his wrists with a box cutter. But this seems like more than a mental exercise. I feel like this Craig kid was trying to take charge of his life. Like me.

As I turn the page again, I hear a noise. I look over at my desk, and the lamp is flickering. But there's something else. I set the notebook down and go over there. A #2 pencil half the size of a new one—I am constantly sharpening my pencils—is, well, it's vibrating. I go to touch it, and, I kid you not, it flies across the desk and lands in the trash can. I reach down and pick it up. Nothing. Just a normal pencil.

Lying on the bed again, I turn the page and find a picture of a creature with red eyes and sharp teeth. Another monster, I guess. All around him are those same tiny monsters, which are floating. I can't believe Craig had drawn these things. Seriously, they are really good. Maybe he was a gifted artist who the other kids liked to pick on.

There was this eighth-grader, Shawna Davis, who was a really good artist. She moved away. I remember she used to make all these cool drawings for the school paper. Apparently, the other eighth-grade girls hated her, and they would spread rumors about her being a big ol' slut. They still talk about her like that sometimes, even though she's long gone. "Slutty Shawna." I think one of them even made up a song. That's what kids do when they find out you're good at something—they make up songs.

Below the hideous monster's picture are words that are hard to pronounce. The page's title reads, NEED THE POWER. I try sounding out the words, but they're difficult.

I've seen Latin before, and these words don't look familiar. One time, our English teacher Mr. Korn brought in a copy of *The Iliad* in the original Greek, so we could see the language Homer wrote in. But this writing doesn't look like Greek. I don't know what it is. Maybe Craig invented his own monster language? I spend the next half-hour trying to sound out the words, but it's no good.

In the end, I'm a little disappointed, but not very. Truth be told, it's not like I really care about any of this. What I mean to say is, I'm not *desperate*. Not like this Craig kid. Who gives a crap about Kirk Wardell, anyways? I'll survive him. Shit, but then I start thinking about the rest of middle school and how I'm going to have to put up with his stupid bullshit, day after day after day. And what about Ollie? He has it worse because he's smaller than me. It would be nice to have an edge for once.

Who am I kidding? It's not worth it. Besides, it's late. I shove the notebook under my bed, brush my teeth, and turn out the light. I can hear Beth on the phone, laughing in this unnatural cartoon voice. That usually means she's talking to a guy. Maybe he's her boyfriend. I wouldn't know because she never tells me anything. I ignore her and go to sleep.

I don't usually remember my dreams, and tonight is no exception. But when I wake up the next morning, I feel funny. Like something has changed.

KIRK, Lonnie, and Gilbert pull one of their usual pranks on me and Ollie in PE—this time, stuffing our gym clothes in the toilet. Real original. And the teacher never says anything. He's too busy checking out the more mature girls in the class. I thought about reporting him one time, but what good would that do? He's married with two young kids. They'll be the ones who end up getting hurt.

Normally, I try and ignore Kirk and his friends because I know I won't see them again for the rest of the day since the three of them are in class with the Special Ed kids. But today, I find myself wishing Craig's list was real, and that I could take care of those thugs once and for all. Not kill them or anything—I only want to hurt them enough so they'll leave me and Ollie alone. Fat chance.

Kirk has us up against the wall now outside the gym, and he's threatening to punch our faces in for no good reason. He calls Ollie a fairy and says I'm trailer trash. Which is kind of funny because Kirk is as poor as me. He was held back—that's why he's so huge. I would say his life is of the typical variety you can find anywhere in this town. He lives in a crappy house with a stepfather who drinks and hits Kirk's mother just about every night. The damned cops are over there all the time.

Wait, how the hell do I know this? Kirk has never once said anything to me about his family, and Lonnie and Gilbert never talk either. But somehow I *know*. I can see the bruises on his mother's face and arms, and I can hear his father cussing at her.

"Sorry about your mom."

"What?" he says.

"I understand she had to go to the emergency room this time. Must've been pretty bad."

Kirk has this strange look on his face. Instead of hitting me, he just stands there, staring at the ground. Lonnie comes up to him and, crouching down and wearing a stupid grin, looks up at his face.

"Dude, you crying?"

Then the big, stupid prick walks away, just like that. His

minions punch both me and Ollie in the arm, and suddenly, we're alone.

"Was all that true?" Ollie says. "What you said about his mom?"

"Yeah."

"But how?"

"I have no idea."

Walking home, I think about Kirk some more, even though I don't want to. It's like my brain has tuned into a new channel, and all this information is pouring in. Ollie is next to me, babbling about something or other. I don't even hear him.

My house is a palace compared to Kirk's place, where all of the furniture is either torn or broken. There's dog pee on the carpet, and the walls are full of holes from where the old man punches it when he isn't whaling on his wife. The backyard is nothing but weeds. There's an unused tool shed toward the back. Kirk likes to hide behind it and whack it. Sometimes, Lonnie and Gilbert join him, and they all imagine they're doing it with high school girls and…

"Ivan!"

Ollie and I are standing in front of his house—I don't even remember arriving. My friend looks pissed.

"Are you even listening?" he says.

"Sure."

"Then why haven't you answered me?"

"I don't know."

"I asked if you wanted to go to Gasher's Park."

"Not today, Ollie. I don't feel well."

AT HOME, everything is same old, same old. Mom is busy making dinner—some disgusting meatless casserole she found on the back of a box of au gratin potatoes or whatever. Beth is at a friend's house, apparently, and Dad is out "looking for work," which usually means he's hanging out downtown with the other unemployed dads over at the Tap 'N' Chat.

Dad's okay, though. He isn't a mean drunk or anything —not like Kirk's stepdad—and he's never laid a finger on Mom or me or Beth, for that matter. In fact, Dad is a major practical joker. I remember one time when he left a fake human head in the refrigerator. You could hear my mom's screams for miles. Another time, he filled one of Beth's bras with shaving cream. Totally inappropriate, but funny as hell. Last year, he hot-glued my science book to my desk. I don't believe in God, but if I did, I would thank him for my old man—job or no job.

After my homework is done, I bring out the notebook. The monster circle on the first page has moved again. I ignore it, turn the page, and review the list. So, this will blow your mind. The first item on the list—NEED THE POWER—is now blood red, while the rest of the items are still black. Had I made it through the first step already? I suppose I thought I wanted the power, but when did I decide I *needed* it?

I'm a little nervous as I turn the page again and silently read the chant below the monster's face. I can feel an invisible hand pressing against my chest. Probably my imagination. But this time, the words are glowing—dude, they actually *glow*. Now, my left hand starts to feel funny, like it itches. I hold it up to look at it and almost fall off the bed.

There's a faint outline of something on my palm! It looks like someone carved it into my hand with an X-Acto knife.

I almost lose my shit and race out of my room into the bathroom, where I blast the hot water into the sink and lather up my palm with soap. Almost burning myself to death, I try scrubbing the mark to get it off. But it's not going away. I keep at it, and finally, the symbol fades. My hand looks like a cooked lobster, so I run cold water over it and hope for the best.

When I return to my room, I find the notebook lying open on my bed where I left it. *Ivan, you idiot!* Mom might've walked in and found it. Anyways, I decide that enough is enough. Kirk isn't worth it. So, I grab the thing and run downstairs, taking the steps two at a time. No one's around. I slip out the back and cram the notebook toward the bottom of the garbage can, under a bag.

So much for being a badass.

IT'S MORNING NOW, and I am lying in bed after a night of zero sleep. For the few minutes I did manage to doze off, I had a terrifying dream, which involved me following Kirk into his backyard. We're walking behind the shed, and I'm starting to get nervous because I think he's going to whip it out. Instead, he points to something hidden in the grass next to the broken-down wooden fence.

It's a baby sparrow.

When I look up, I can see a nest in the orange tree. There are other babies in it, and the mom bird is sitting on a branch, watching us. Kirk grins at the mom bird—only he's not Kirk anymore. He's some other kid I've never seen before, with dark beady eyes, super-short red hair, and bad skin. He picks up the baby bird with both hands and, chanting something I can't understand, crushes it in his fingers, the blood dripping onto the dead grass and burning it like acid.

"Ivan, are you up yet?" It's Mom calling from downstairs.

"Yeah!"

I realize it's late, but I don't feel like moving. Though I don't want to, I raise my left hand and examine the palm. Nothing—except the skin is still a little red from all that hot water. Could the mark have been my imagination? Creepy shit like this happens in movies all the time, but not in actual life. I remember one time when me and Ollie were playing around with one of those cheesy Ouija boards. And guess what—*nothing happened*. Those things are bogus if you ask me. Just the same, I'm glad I threw the notebook away.

No time to shower, so I brush my teeth and dress. As I reach down to grab my backpack, I see something sticking out a little ways under my bed. No, it can't be. Shutting my eyes tight, I get down on my knees. When I open them, I can see it lying there.

It's the damned notebook!

I'm pretty shaken now as I leave my bedroom. I decide the best thing is to return the notebook to Craig's locker. As I pass the bathroom, I can see my sister putting on her makeup.

"Hey, Ivan?" she says. "What was all that noise last night?"

"What noise?"

She leans over the sink, smacks her lips in the mirror, pushes up her boobs, and walks out. I'm guessing she's meeting her boyfriend at school.

"I don't know," she says. "It was like you were moaning or something. I thought maybe you were, you know…"

"What? Shut the hell up. I had a bad dream, is all. And since when do you listen to what goes on in my room?"

"I don't, dumbass, but you woke me up." She starts down the stairs.

"Hey, Beth? Do you remember what time that was?"

"Like three? How should I know?"

Okay, so I've seen enough horror movies to know that three a.m. is the witching hour. And people have been known to do some crazy shit during that time. Like the pharmacist who used to live on the next block. Last year—for no good reason, apparently—he decided to cut up his wife and baby daughter with a chainsaw and stick all the pieces in a freezer in the garage. He said it was because of an occult book he'd bought at a yard sale. But the cops said it was because of all the drugs he'd been stealing from the Rite Aid where he worked. And the jury agreed.

My point is, me having a nightmare during the witching hour was just a stupid coincidence. There's no way I am blaming that on a notebook I found in some kid's locker. That's crazy talk. Still…

"SO WHATEVER HAPPENED to that notebook you found?" Ollie says.

We're almost at school, and all I can think about is how I'm going to get through another day of the Kirk Wardell shit show.

"I took it. That's all."

"What? Why?"

"Curious, I guess."

"Ivan, you needa put it back."

"I hope I can."

"What do you mean?"

"Ollie, I wasn't going to tell you, but there's something weird about that notebook. Last night, I tried throwing it away, but it showed up in my room again."

"Oh, come on. It was prob'ly your dad playing another joke."

"Also, there's this mark on my hand." I showed him my palm.

"I don't see anything."

"That's because I washed it off. But it was there, I swear."

"What else?"

"I had this really bad dream. And I know things now—things about Kirk that no one ever told me."

"You mean like, about his mom?"

"Yeah."

"Dude, you needa lose that book."

While Ollie is getting his books, I sneak back through the gate and approach Craig's locker. I'm thinking I can throw the notebook in real fast and leave, with no one the wiser. But when I get there, I can see that the door is shut. Just as I'm about to open it, stupid Hershey shows up.

"Hey!" he says. "What'd I tell you?"

He pushes me away and checks the locker. If he opens it, he'll see that I took the notebook. Better to walk away now.

"So did you do it?" Ollie says.

"No. Hershey caught me. Look, it's no big deal. I'll wait till after school."

As Ollie and I head to class, I can see Kirk in the parking lot. He's standing there with his stepdad, and he looks butthurt about something—probably his mom. They're having a loud argument, and people are staring. Kirk says something to him, and his stepdad takes a swipe at the kid's head, almost knocking him down. But Kirk doesn't do anything—he just takes it.

My dad had told me one time a lot of guys in this town grew up like Kirk. When they turned eighteen, their fathers threw them out of the house. It was like they thought they'd done their job, and now they were going to kick back, get drunk, and watch porn. The thing of it is, when these "model parents" got old, their sons never came back to see them. Never gave them money or looked after them when they got sick.

"Lonely old bastards," Dad had said. "And now they just sit in their houses alone, waiting to die. Wondering what they did to deserve this."

I don't know why, but it occurs to me that this is the reason why our neighbor Luckman is so mean and keeps taking it out on the dog.

Mr. Charbonneau is walking across the parking lot now. I watch as Kirk's stepdad jumps into his faded, beat-up Toyota truck and peels out. The principal says something to Kirk, who's still standing there, trying not to cry. Then the kid walks away without saying anything. I can tell he's super pissed.

I guess me and Ollie will get ours later.

KIRK DIDN'T COME to PE and, as a result, Lonnie and Gilbert left us alone. Me and Ollie ate lunch at a corner table in the cafeteria, and when we didn't see Kirk there either, we figured we were home free. I still planned on getting rid of the notebook and hoped I could slip it into Craig's locker after school without anyone seeing me. Ollie agreed to be a lookout, in case Hershey showed up. Later, we would go to Gasher's Park and ride our skateboards. No such luck.

There's this girl, right? Regina Sanchez. She transferred into our district last year, and I got to see her through most of sixth grade, though I never talked to her or anything back then. Anyways, I sort of like her now.

She's hella cute, and I can't be sure, but I think she might like me too a little bit.

I never talk about Regina to Ollie because there's no one who's interested in him yet, and I don't want him feeling bad and stuff. I didn't think anyone knew about my interest in Regina. But then after school, I see Kirk talking to her across from the chain link fence, and I know something's up.

Ollie is meeting with Mr. Ryan about his math homework, so I'm all alone. I'm just about to sneak in and return the notebook to Craig's locker when Lonnie and Gilbert appear on either side of me—where in hell did they come from? Lonnie grabs my arms and pulls them hard behind me as Gilbert undoes my jeans and pulls them down around my ankles. Then he does the same with my underwear.

Everything is happening so fast; I don't even scream. I'm kicking and trying to get away, but Lonnie and Gilbert have me pressed up against the fence. If there was ever a worse nightmare, I can't think of it. At least most of the other kids have gone home already. Now, Kirk is laughing and pointing. Then Regina sees me. Seriously, I want to die. But instead of laughing, her face turns dark red, and she runs away.

"Stupid bitch!" Kirk says, angry as hell. "You were supposed to laugh!"

I never thought I'd be glad to see Hershey. When he comes around the corner with his cart, the two assholes see him and take off. Hershey walks over fast and parks his cart in front of me to give me some privacy.

"This Kirk Wardell's doing?" he says.

"Yeah." I'm buckling my belt now as I step around the cart.

"He's garbage. But his old man's worse."

"Thanks."

I'm trying hard not to cry. The last thing I need is for the school janitor to feel sorry for me. Hershey is saying something else now, but I'm too busy replaying the incident in my head like a movie clip—especially Regina's reaction. And then I realize she didn't laugh at me. I guess that's something. Still, I'm not sure I can ever face her again.

"Better get home now," Hershey says.

I decide not to wait for Ollie. On the way to my house, I pass the 7-Eleven. Kirk, Lonnie, and Gilbert are inside. It looks like they're giving the old black dude who works there some shit. And then, the anger I was feeling before rises. Tears spring from my eyes, and I feel like screaming. Next thing I know, I'm standing in the alley behind the store, reading Craig's notebook.

ABSORB THE POWER.

Craig had drawn a life-size picture of a hand with a strange symbol on the palm. It looks kind of like an eye, and it's dark red. I don't know what I'm supposed to do, so I try and figure it out. It looks like if I put my left hand on top of the picture, it will fit perfectly. So that's what I do. Then I sound out the words below the picture. At first, nothing happens. But on the third try, a sharp pain shoots through my hand and up my arm, causing me to drop the notebook. As I reach down to pick it up, I hear footsteps coming toward me.

"Hey, look, guys," someone says. I recognize Lonnie's voice. "I think Stein wants to whip it out again. Maybe we should help him."

I'm gripping the notebook hard now, and when I look at those three losers, they freeze, all the color leaving their faces. Then they turn around and walk away. I have no idea what just happened, but on the way home, all I can think about is the notebook and getting to the next item on the list.

"HOW WAS SCHOOL TODAY?" Mom says.

"Another perfect day."

Dad and Beth are out again, so it's just the two of us for dinner. I love my mom, but sometimes, I don't feel like talking. She's always asking me about my "plans" and my feelings and stuff. At this point, I'm just playing with my food, not saying anything. When I look up at her, I can see she looks sad.

Mom married my dad when she was only nineteen, so the story goes. Her parents were "lower middle class," which in this town meant you were one notch above trailer trash. I think she did it to get out of the house and give her younger sister, Allison, a chance. My aunt wanted to go to college, and I guess Mom figured with one less mouth to feed, maybe their parents would be able to swing it. Aunt Allison ended up with a full ride to the state university. Mom said she was so happy for her, but I think deep down she would have liked to go, too.

My mom used to work at Walmart, but they had a bunch of layoffs because of the economy. Then Dad got laid off, and everything went to hell. We had to sell one of our cars and cancel our cable subscription. Fortunately, both my parents are really good savers.

"I'm sorry you don't like dinner," she says.

I can tell by her voice she thinks this is her fault. So, I scoop up a huge glob of instant mashed potatoes, pack them into my mouth, and grin like an idiot, which makes her laugh. And just to prove her wrong, I eat everything on the plate.

After finishing my homework, I'm sitting on the bed, going through the notebook again. None of the words from the list are glowing now, but as I turn the pages, my palm is starting to feel funny again. I stop at the page with the title ABSORB THE POWER. The picture of the hand is different. I keep looking at it, and as I do, the itching turns into pain. And then I realize the symbol is missing. I turn my left hand over. Now I can see that same symbol on my palm! This is seriously freaking me out. *Calm down, Ivan. Just breathe.*

I'm not sure when I fell asleep, but when I open my eyes, I'm lying on my bed in the dark. My hand isn't hurting as much. I can tell it's late, and as I lie there quietly, I can hear Beth's voice next door through the wall. It sounds like she's whispering something over and over.

"Beth?"

The whispering becomes louder. Then I hear the words clearly; only they're not coming from Beth's room at all. The voice—which is not hers—is speaking right next to me.

"Kill them all," it says.

I'M REALLY nauseous this morning, and my head is pounding. Ollie notices as we walk to school.

"You look terrible," he says.

"Thanks."

"How come you didn't wait for me yesterday?"

"There was sort of an incident." I didn't want to talk about it.

"So, I guess you're too sick to go to Gasher's Park today?"

"I don't know, Ollie. Ask me later, okay?"

I make sure to keep my left hand tucked inside my hoodie pocket. I don't want anyone seeing that symbol and thinking I'm a freak. When we arrive at school, Ollie heads straight for his locker. I can see Regina walking toward me. I try going the other way.

"Ivan?" she says.

I stop and slowly turn around. Might as well get it over with. She's so pretty and so sweet. And I hate Kirk so much for ruining that for me.

"Hi."

"I'm sorry about yesterday," she says.

"So am I."

"And I didn't think it was funny at all. Because it wasn't, Ivan. It was cruel."

"Regina, I…"

"I like you, Ivan. Do you think we can just forget about it?"

I don't know what else to do, so I give her a hug, which makes her giggle. Then she pecks me on the cheek and steps back, smiling, her cheeks flushed.

"Maybe we could get an ice cream sometime?" she says.

"That would be amazing."

"Oh, your hand!"

"What?"

I had forgotten about that. Too late—she's holding my hand now and examining it like the school nurse.

"Does it hurt?" she says.

"I don't…"

"It's really red."

I take my hand back and look at it. Nothing; no symbol. "It's a little sore. I burned it on the stove last night."

The warning bell rings, and Regina heads off to class in the opposite direction from me and Ollie.

"Maybe you should transfer into Honors," he says as we beat it to class. "Then you could see her all the time."

"What about you?"

"Well, we still have Gasher's Park."

"I'll think about it, Ollie."

NOT EVEN KIRK WARDELL could ruin what turned out to be a perfect day. In PE, he keeps his distance. Lonnie and Gilbert continue picking on Ollie, though. When I confront them, they back off.

At lunch, I can hear people talking about "the incident." Some are laughing and pointing at me—mostly the guys—but I don't care. After me and Ollie get our food, we pick a table in the middle of the cafeteria. I can see Kirk lurking in a corner, watching me like a pit bull who's about to bite. He'll get his soon.

After school, me and Ollie run home to get our skateboards. I haven't felt sick all day. If anything, I'm feeling stronger. When we get to Gasher's Park, I notice a couple other middle school kids riding around in the skate park. So, we join them and make the most of our time before the high schoolers show up. Afterwards, Ollie buys us all ice cream from the truck. As I'm eating mine, I think about Regina. Then I start thinking of ways I can earn some cash so I can buy her an ice cream.

AFTER DINNER, I'm sitting on my bed and staring at the notebook. It all becomes clear to me now. If I want to be happy, I need to get Kirk and his loser friends out of the way for good. Once I do that, I won't need the notebook anymore. Besides, I would be helping Ollie, too. Craig must've come to the same conclusion, which is why he created the book in the first place.

I turn to the page TEST THE POWER and find a drawing of a scrawny, bald kid standing in the center of a forest, holding up his left hand like he's showing it to someone. Craig had drawn these bright rays coming out. I can't see who he's showing his hand to, though.

I'm pretty stoked now and stand in the center of my room, holding up my hand. I'm facing the sliding closet doors, which have mirrors on them because this used to be Beth's room. I read the words out loud. At first, nothing happens. Then my hand feels like it's getting hot. I hear a whooshing noise, and a second later one of the mirrors cracks. I realize Mom will kill me when she sees what I've done. So instead of practicing anymore in my bedroom, I decide to go outside.

"Mom?"

She's standing over the kitchen sink, rinsing off the last of the dinner dishes. Our dishwasher is busted, and since we can't afford to fix it, Mom has to wash everything by hand.

"Yes, honey?"

"Isn't tomorrow trash day?"

"Uh-huh."

"Well, I thought I'd take the cans out to the curb."

She stares at me like I'm three kinds of crazy. Then she smiles. It's been a long time since she smiled like that.

"Ivan, thank you for volunteering. Let me get some more trash together, and you can take everything out, okay?"

"Sure thing."

"What'cha got there?" she says, pointing at the notebook.

"Just some notes. I'm studying for a test."

Though I wasn't even trying to, I must have scored some major brownie points. All I had wanted was to find a logical excuse to go outside. Whatever. My plan had worked.

Standing in the backyard, I open the notebook and turn to a page with another picture of the bald kid. This time, he's standing on a deserted road, his hand raised up, and he's surrounded by dead animals, all lying in a circle. Though the picture is disturbing, it doesn't bother me.

I decide to try out my new powers on Luckman's cat, who likes to hang around our yard for some reason. The animal is ancient. The fur around its face used to be black, but now it's gray. Also, it has a goofy eye, which is all clouded up. It always reminds me of the old man who gets himself killed in "The Tell-Tale Heart." Whenever the cat sees me, it makes a low maowing noise and rubs against my pant leg. I don't mind, I guess. But as a rule, I don't like cats.

It takes me, like, one minute to roll each trash can out to the curb. The whole time, the cat is following me, purring like one of those toy drones. When I'm finished, I return to the backyard and look up at the sky. Normally, you can't see anything in this neighborhood—too many lights—but tonight I can make out all kinds of stars. And they're really bright.

When I look down again, the cat is lying on its back in front of me, hoping for a belly scratch. I usually avoid any display of affection, but this time, I crouch down and go to work. As I stroke the thing up and down its stomach, it purrs even louder and kneads the air with its paws.

Finally, I've had enough and stand up straight. My hand is hurting, and when I look at it, I can see that symbol has reappeared on my palm, only darker. Do you remember the scene from *Raiders of the Lost Ark*, where the evil Nazi dude tries to remove the medallion from the fire and burns his hand? Then later in the desert when he gives the ol' "Heil Hitler," the medallion's face is permanently etched on his hand in scar tissue? Well, that's what this thing looks like. And it hurts. Bad.

Before I can think about what I'm doing, I step back, raise my hand in front of me, and aiming it at the cinder block wall, I read the words. Nothing; not even a fizzle. All of a sudden, this voice in my head says to concentrate on the cat, which is sitting a little ways off, licking its front paw.

I tell myself I'm just going to give it a little shock. As I raise my hand, I can feel the air around me becoming all staticky. Then a white jet of electricity passes between me and the cat. The animal jumps, like, ten feet and, screeching, tears off toward its yard.

"Ivan?" It's my mom, calling me from the house.

"Yeah, coming!"

I don't think any more about the cat.

———

THE NEXT MORNING when I walk outside, the garbage men are next door. Luckman is carrying a black garbage bag and limping toward the sidewalk. He got his leg shot up pretty bad in Vietnam, and they had to amputate it. Now he wears this fake aluminum thing. Dad told me once he's in pain all the time and likes to "self-medicate," which would explain all those empty Early Times bottles in the trash every week.

"Hey," my neighbor says. "Any problem if I throw in a dead cat?"

One of the men shrugs and takes the bag from him. I don't know; Luckman could've killed the cat, for all I know

—he's a mean, peglegged son of a bitch who beats his dog without mercy. But who am I kidding? As we walk to school, I don't say anything to Ollie about murdering my neighbor's cat. My friend wouldn't understand.

Kirk is absent from school today, apparently, which means Dumb and Dumber will leave me and Ollie alone since they're basically pussies on their own. I think maybe he senses I'm getting stronger, even though I haven't made it all the way through the list yet. Or maybe he's sick at home. Something tells me, though, he isn't done torturing us, especially now that I know stuff about his mom.

Before leaving for school today, I'd gotten out the notebook and looked up the next thing on the list—AFFIRM THE POWER. It seemed I was supposed to offer a sacrifice. The notebook didn't say exactly what, but the picture Craig had drawn showed the bald kid standing over a rickety table, lowering a hunting knife onto his right pinky. Gross. I decided there and then there was no way I was going to cut off my own finger. So, I threw the notebook back under my bed and hoped Mom wouldn't find it when she vacuumed my room.

After school, me and Ollie run home to get our skateboards, then head over to Gasher's Park. The sky looks strange. It's all overcast like it's going to rain, but instead of it being gray, the clouds are *yellow*. I should have known something was up and gone home. But we're too excited because the high schoolers aren't anywhere in sight, and we have the whole place to ourselves.

We're just getting into it when the king of the douches Franklin shows up and stares at us as we skate around, laughing and fake-punching each other. His missing eye is completely bandaged up—he looks like the freakin' Mummy. When he sees us, he kind of looks *past us* like there's something else in the skate park.

"Hey!" he says.

Ollie falls off his board, and suddenly, I have a bad feeling about the whole thing. There isn't anyone else around, not even those other middle schoolers. And we can't run away because Franklin is blocking the only exit. So, we stand close together and wait to see what this major dickwad will do.

Franklin opens the gate and walks in. I notice he doesn't even have his skateboard, and I wonder what he's thinking. It doesn't take long to find out. He reaches into his pocket and pulls out a butterfly knife. I can't believe it. Is this psycho actually going to cut up a couple kids?

"You know what sucks?" he says. "Bad luck. And bad luck is what I've had since you two showed up here."

"It's not our fault you lost your eye, Franklin. Didn't anyone ever tell you not to drink and drive?"

I should've kept my mouth shut. He's marching toward us now. Me and Ollie split up, so at least he won't be able to hurt us both. Maybe one of us can make it to the gate and call 911.

Ollie was always a terrible runner. I reach the gate in no time, but when I turn around, I see Franklin coming at my friend with the knife. Ollie is just standing there, waving his hands in front of him and ordering Franklin to leave him alone.

"Ollie, get out of there!"

Without thinking, I raise my left hand. But I'm not quick enough, and Franklin swipes the knife across Ollie's throat. I watch as my best friend in the whole world grabs his neck and falls to the ground, bright blood squirting through his fingers.

"No!"

A kind of blinding hate takes over as I aim my throbbing hand at Franklin. He glares at me, still holding the bloody knife. With his other hand, he tears at his throat like he's having trouble breathing. In another second, he drops the knife and sinks to his knees, his head whipping back and forth like it no longer wants to be attached to his body. I keep my hand steady, though, and, feeling a surge of power leaving me, I watch as Franklin's screams turn into tiny chirping noises.

Scared now, I try and lower my hand, but I can't—something won't let me. This time, there isn't any electricity. I hear a loud crack, and Franklin's head pops off his body like some invisible force tore it free. His arms are windmilling and, as his head hits the ground and rolls, a geyser of black blood shoots straight up out his neck. His headless body falls sideways on the ground, right next to Ollie.

When it's over, nothing is moving. Someone must've called 911 because I can hear sirens. I run across the hilly concrete to check on my friend. His eyes are staring straight up at nothing, and he isn't breathing. I really want to stay with him, but something is telling me to get out of there.

I'm crying like a little girl when Mom opens the front door—I can't help it. She asks me what happened, and I tell her some low-life killed Ollie, and the cops came and everything. She tries to comfort me, but it's no good. I can't stop thinking about my friend.

When Dad walks into the kitchen, she says, "Ed, we have to call the police."

"We will. Let's let him calm down."

They continue talking, but I don't hear them anymore. Then I remember something and crawl off to my room. I take out the notebook and flip to the last page I looked at. Instead of the drawing of the bald kid cutting off his finger, I now see an image of a boy who looks a lot like Ollie lying on a black altar, dead.

Once I realize what I've done—I mean, really think about it—I spend the next few minutes in the bathroom, puking up my guts. My best friend is dead. And that one-eyed freak show killed him. Then the truth hits me—*I* killed Ollie. Not on purpose, but as a sacrifice to whatever evil power Craig had unleashed through his list. I have to get rid of the book.

MY PARENTS SAID I could stay home from school today. The sound of strange voices wakes me up. Curious, I get dressed and walk downstairs. Two men in blue suits are sitting with my parents in the living room, asking all kinds of questions about what happened at the skate park. I wish I could sneak out the back, but Dad has already seen me and waves me over.

"This is my son, Ivan," he says. "Ivan, these detectives are here to ask about what happened yesterday."

"Why don't you sit down?" Mom says.

"I don't want to."

"We'll try to be brief," the larger of the two detectives says, smiling at me through brown teeth. "Did you know the deceased, Franklin Rogers?"

"I…I've seen him at the skate park."

"And did you see him yesterday afternoon, around four p.m.?"

"Yes."

As the cop questions me, his partner writes down everything I say. I know they're going to ask me about how Franklin died. There's no way I'm telling them the truth.

"Ivan, can you describe what happened yesterday afternoon?"

I look at my parents and start crying again, which turns out to be a good thing because it makes them nervous. Mom gets up and takes my hand.

"He killed my friend."

"You mean, Franklin?" the cop says.

"Yeah. Franklin killed my friend Ollie."

"And you witnessed this?"

"Yes."

"How did he kill him?"

I didn't want to think about what I saw—Ollie lying on the concrete, bleeding out. But I owed it to him.

"Franklin cut his throat with, with a butterfly knife."

"Okay. And had he ever threatened you or your friend before?"

"All the time. He and his friends hated us coming into the skate park."

"His friends. Were they there, too?"

"No, just Franklin."

"I see. And what happened after he attacked your friend?"

"I ran."

"So you didn't see what happened to Franklin Rogers?"

"No. Did something happen?"

Both detectives look at my parents, and the room goes quiet. I'm worried they know what I did.

"Ivan," Dad says. "Franklin is dead."

"What?"

"We can't explain how it happened," the big detective says, "but he was decapitated. Do you know what that means, son?"

This goes on for, like, another half-hour. The cop asks whether I think Franklin might have had enemies. *Franklin.*

Why are they so interested in him? Just because his head came off like the cork on a champagne bottle, that's no reason to give a flying crap about some loser who was better off dead. Ollie was the one who had suffered. Why can't they see that?

"Ivan," the detective says. "Is there anything else you want to tell us?"

"What? No."

"We realize your friend's death has upset you, but I would advise you against withholding information."

"I don't know anything!"

"Detective," Mom says, "can't you see how upset Ivan is about the whole incident?"

"Yes, ma'am. But this a murder investigation, and I'm afraid we're obliged to ask these questions."

He's looking directly at me now, and I suddenly want to tell these two bozos everything—about the locker and Craig's list, and about that crazy old coot of a janitor, Hershey. But all I can do is stare at the cops and say nothing.

"Thanks for everything," the detective in charge says to Mom. Then he and his partner take off.

I know nothing will come of this. Look, I don't watch a lot of television because it bores me, but there's one thing I do know. People get killed every day, and no one *ever* figures out what happened to them. They're here one day and gone the next. That's life. Especially in the town where I live. And if these two detectives have to run around investigating every damn thing that happens around here, what are the chances they'll find out who did it? Zero.

And another thing. Why shouldn't people like Franklin get what's coming to them? What happened to him was his own fault. My friend is dead, and I'm no longer sorry for what I did.

"Are you hungry?" Mom says as she closes the front door.

"I want to go back to my room."

"It's going to be okay, Ivan," Dad says. Then to Mom, "Right, Raylene?"

"Of course it is. You go ahead and get some rest now."

I WOULD NEVER TELL anyone else this because they might think I'm a fairy, but when I'm upset, I like to take a hot bath. It always calms me down. After dinner, I can't wait to climb into the tub upstairs. I run the water, making it as hot as I can stand it, climb in, sit back, and spread a wet washcloth across my face. Then I take a deep breath and shut out the world.

One time, Beth needed to get ready for a date and was banging on the door. That was the day Kirk had thrown my backpack down the muddy hill behind our school after it had rained for like a year. When I tried taking a swing at him, he picked me up and heaved me like a sack of manure. I went sliding all the way down on my stomach. When I got home, Mom had a fit.

Anyways, I was so upset I had forgotten to lock the bathroom door. My stupid sister barged in, and when she saw me naked, she laughed like some kind of idiot. After she'd left, I lay there in the tub for, like, hours and bawled my eyes out.

I don't have to worry about Beth tonight. I made sure to lock the bathroom door. Also, she isn't even home. The hot bath is not working, though. As hard as I try shutting everything out, I keep seeing Ollie in my mind—his eyes staring at nothing. Then I hear a noise. I rip the washcloth off my face, and when I open my eyes, Ollie is standing there next to the bathtub, in the bloody clothes he was wearing at the skate park! His neck is all dark and ragged with dried blood, and he's smiling. I don't get it. Why would you smile if you're dead?

"No, no… Go away, Ollie."

His voice sounds odd like he's talking through the cardboard tube from a roll of paper towels.

"Ivan, I know why you did it, and I don't blame you. I hated Franklin, too. But I needa tell you something important about the notebook."

I stare at him for the longest time, telling myself he isn't real—that it's all in my head—but seeing he's still here, I give in.

No one should ever have to see a dead person talking to them. That's for crazies. The thing is, I'm not even surprised it's happening. And I'm not all that scared. Maybe it's because it's Ollie and not some horrible monster. And I miss him. So I sit up and pretend he's still alive, and we're just having a conversation.

"I appreciate you caring about me and all," I say, "what with you being a ghost. But I have everything under control."

"No, you don't."

"Yes, I do. I've decided to finish the list. Then Kirk and his stupid friends are going to get what's coming to them. And if I have time, I'm going to take care of the rest of those shitlickers at the skate park."

"That's what I'm trying to tell you, Ivan," he says. "You *can't* finish the list."

"Why?"

"Because it doesn't end until you're dead."

"What? How would you know?"

"Look, I'm not a kid anymore. I'm a *soul*—I don't have an age. And I can see things now."

"Dead people?"

"Grown-up things."

I'm starting to feel nervous. "Like what?"

"Bad things, Ivan. Didn't you ever wonder where that notebook came from?"

"Yeah, it belonged to some kid named Craig."

"And weren't you ever curious to know what happened to him?"

"I guess."

"He *died*, Ivan."

"What? No way—it's just a lot of stupid words."

"He died and went to hell."

"How would you know?"

"Because I can see him. He's far away, but I know it's him."

"But how?"

"I'm not really sure. It's like, I can see a whole bunch of people down there. Millions, maybe even *billions*."

Now I'm mad and scared at the same time. I can feel tears rolling down my cheeks. I'm not embarrassed, though, because Ollie is my best friend and has seen me cry lots of times. He never told anyone either, which is what best friends do.

"Well, so what?"

"You needa destroy the notebook," he says.

"How? I tried getting rid of it once, but it came back."

"I don't know. Don't do the last step. After that, it'll be too late."

"What happens if I do?"

"They come for you."

"Who? Ollie, who comes for me?"

"Demons," he says.

"What? I didn't think those things were real."

"They're real, Ivan."

"Jeez, Ollie, I'm really scared."

"I know. I was scared when you went over to that locker. Remember? It was like I felt something was going to happen. It's the reason I ran away."

"Why didn't you tell me?"

"I tried to, but you wouldn't listen. I have to go. There's this thing that happens to you when you're dead. It's like a wind. And it blows you places you don't want to go. I can't control it. I hope it takes me to heaven eventually."

"Ollie, I am so sorry."

"It's okay, Ivan," he says. "I forgive you."

Then like nothing, he vanishes. My heart is ready to come out of my chest; it's pumping so hard. I sit up and lean over the rim of the tub. And what I see on the floor makes me want to scream like the old lady down the street when she learned the cops had shot her son dead in a botched convenience store robbery. I sit there, staring at the only thing on the tile floor that isn't white.

It's Ollie's bloody footprints, redder than anything in the whole world.

BEFORE GOING TO BED, I force myself not to open the notebook—but it's hard. It's like the thing is calling to me. My head is hurting now. Bad. I can hear voices coming from under my bed and out of the walls. At first, they talk nice, telling me about the power and how I will be able to destroy my enemies. When I don't give in, they screech at me, threatening to destroy everyone I care about. I can't make them stop.

I lie on my bed, holding my head in my hands, and try not to scream. No matter what the voices say, though, I ignore them and concentrate on what Ollie told me. I can't do the last step, no matter what. I don't want to go to hell. I just want everyone to leave me alone. I don't remember falling asleep, but when I wake up, it's morning, and the voices have stopped.

After showering and dressing, I shove the notebook into my backpack and run downstairs. Beth is studying at the table. My parents seem surprised to see me.

"Ivan, are you sure you want to go to school today?" Mom says.

"I'm fine."

"I don't want you walking," Dad says.

"What? Why?"

"Beth, can you give your brother a ride?"

"Sure," she says, not looking up.

Mom tries to make me eat breakfast, but I'm not hungry. She keeps asking how I feel, and I tell her I'm okay. Then I head out the door with Beth.

My sister drives an ancient VW bug that still runs, thanks to Dad. The inside always smells like her perfume, but I don't mind.

"So, are you doing okay?" she says.

"I guess."

"Mom and Dad are really worried about you."

"Why?"

"Maybe because they think it could've been you instead of Ollie."

"Beth? What would you do if you could get back at the people that hurt you?"

"You mean, like revenge?"

"Yeah."

"I remember my ninth-grade English teacher had this quote up on her wall. I thought it was pretty cool. '*Before you embark on a journey of revenge, dig two graves.*'"

"What does it mean?"

"It means one of the graves is for you, Ivan."

"Shit."

I don't say anything else the rest of the way.

WHEN I GET TO SCHOOL, I can see Kirk and his buddies waiting for me. I'm tempted to use the power, but instead, I pretend to ignore them as the warning bell rings.

"Heard your girlfriend got killed," he says.

"Leave me alone, Kirk."

"So were you two queer for each other?"

I can feel the notebook in my backpack pressing down on me like a pile of bricks. I want so much to complete the last step on the list and take care of these bitches once and for all, but I remember Ollie's warning. Kirk isn't worth it. Then something pops into my head, and I smile to myself.

"How's your mom, by the way? Must've upset her, finding out the old man's been sticking it to that Asian stripper over at the motel by the truck stop."

Before Kirk can answer me, I bolt, making it to my classroom just as the final bell rings. Most likely, he'll be waiting for me after school. But I have other plans. As soon as I can sneak out, I'm going over to the weed lot behind the Valero station and burning the damned notebook. I have it all figured out. I'll dig a shallow grave in the dirt and, using the kitchen matches I stole, I'll destroy Craig's list once and for all. That's the plan, anyways.

I hate it when teachers act all sympathetic and stuff. They get this "concerned" look and talk to you in a soft voice. And they smile a lot. They think they're helping, but this does nothing but call attention to the whole situation. I just want everyone to leave me alone. Halfway through second period, the voices start up again. I can't hear what the teacher is saying, so I keep my eyes down and doodle. My head feels like someone is smashing it with a hammer. And now the other kids are starting to stare like they can hear the voices, too. Then everything goes dark.

———

WHEN I OPEN MY EYES, the school nurse is staring down at me, and I realize I'm lying on a cot in her office.

"Feeling better?" she says.

I sit up and look around. The room is empty except for the two of us. A steady ticking is coming from an old Felix the Cat pendulum clock hanging on the wall, which she must've gotten off eBay. The eyes and tail move with every click.

"What happened?"

She smiles and pats my hand, which I don't mind. She's old—maybe fifty—and wears glasses with pink frames. Her hair is gray and pulled back. Her breath smells like spearmint gum. I don't know why, but she reminds me of my grandma. She's dead.

"You passed out, Ivan. What's the last thing you remember?"

"I was in history class. Wait, I heard something."

"A noise?"

I refuse to tell her it was the voices from the notebook. "It's probably nothing. My head hurts so much. Where's my backpack?"

"It's right here. Listen, I'm concerned about something."

She shows me a sheet of lined notebook paper. On it is a drawing of a pit. And inside, hands are reaching up. It's not very good, but there's something about it that makes me want to look away.

"What is that?"

"Don't you remember?" she says. "It's what you were drawing when you passed out."

"Please, just throw it away."

She crumples it up. "I called your dad. He'll be here soon."

Now I'm scared. For as long as I can remember, my dad had never picked me up from school. Was Mom sick? There's a knock at the door. I see my father standing in the doorway, unshaven and wearing an old T-shirt with a paint stain on it. Way to make an impression, Dad. He looks worried, which makes me even more scared, and I can tell something is wrong at home.

"Hey, buddy," he says. "Come on. I'll take you home." Then to the nurse, "Guess he's still upset about his friend."

"Of course," the nurse says. "I'll sign him out." Then to me, "Take care, Ivan. Be sure to rest. Everything's going to be okay."

But I know it isn't going to be okay. Ollie had warned me, but maybe it's already too late. Craig is taking over my life. I have to get rid of the notebook. Tonight, I tell myself on the ride home. I'll do it tonight.

"How's Mom?"

"Why do you ask?" Dad says.

"I don't know. I thought she would pick me up."

"She'll be fine."

"What do you mean? What happened?"

Dad doesn't say anything for several blocks. Maybe he's trying to think up a good lie. At a red light, he looks at me, more serious than I've ever seen him.

"She had an accident with a kitchen knife," he says.

"What!"

"Ivan, calm down. She's fine. I drove her to the emergency room, and they stitched her right up. She's resting. We're having pizza for dinner. You love pizza, right?"

This was the notebook's fault—I knew it. Though Dad didn't say anything about her, I wonder now if my sister is also in danger. And what about him? What, my whole family is about to get it because I'm refusing to finish the list? It's not fair!

We're close to my house now, and the voices have started up again. They sound like tiny foreign words blowing toward me on the same wind that's sending Ollie all over hell and back. Some of the voices are angry, and others sad. Are these the voices of other kids who read Craig's list and died? I don't want to find out. Instead of listening to them, I squeeze my eyes shut and try and think of something else. Luckily, Dad turns on the radio to an alternative rock station. Trying to be relevant, I guess.

DAD HAD ORDERED MY FAVORITE, pepperoni and mushroom. I'm not even hungry, though. But I don't want my parents to get suspicious, so I force down a slice and chug a glass of cold milk. The food is sitting in my stomach like a rock. I feel like hurling. But I have to appear normal till I can sneak out of the house later.

Mom doesn't look too bad. Her right hand is bandaged, and she's eating with her left. Dad gives her another slice and cuts it up to make it easier for her. I'm pretty sure they still love each other, even after all the bad luck.

"Mom, does it hurt much?"

"It's so stupid, Ivan," she says. "It was like the knife flew out of my hand. Guess I wasn't paying attention."

Dad shakes his head. "I've always said those knives were too sharp."

My sister looks at me sympathetically and touches my hand. Totally unlike her.

"You okay, Ivan?"

"Yeah. I think I'm just tired."

The room becomes darker suddenly, but no one else seems to notice. Beth has turned into a creature with red eyes and a forked tongue. And her voice sounds like someone sawing through a metal pipe. She's squeezing my hand so tight; I want to scream. When I look down, she has claws instead of fingers, and they're digging into my skin and drawing blood.

"Finish the list, Ivan," she says in that metallic voice, "or I'll slaughter everyone here. Except you, of course. You, I want to live so you can spend the rest of your stinking shit life listening to the wretched voices of your family roasting in hell. Mom, Dad, and that ripe sow Beth. There's a good boy."

I shut my eyes tight, and when I open them again, everything is normal. Beth is telling Mom and Dad a funny story about cheerleading practice, and they're laughing. I need to get out of here before I explode.

"Can I be excused?"

Mom looks at me. "I'm worried about you, Ivan."

"I'm okay. Really. It's just that I have a lot of home-work tonight."

"Try to go to bed early," Dad says.

I get up from the table and kiss Mom on the cheek. I don't know why I did it, but it seemed like the right thing to do.

INSTEAD OF DOING HOMEWORK, I'm sitting in my room, staring at the wall. The voices have started up again —taunting me—but I'm choosing to ignore them the way I choose to ignore the pounding in my head and the fact that my stomach is jackhammering. The things on the list I completed made me stronger—able to harm my enemies. But they also gave me the strength to resist. And that's just what I'm doing.

Nothing is going to keep me from destroying the note-book. I wish I could see Ollie one more time so I could tell him. I still can't believe he's gone. Everything that happened was because of the evil in that notebook. And I wonder now if this kind of bad exists in the world, then does that mean God exists, too?

It's almost ten o'clock. The house is quiet. I open my bedroom window and stare out at the big oak tree, whose branches don't quite reach close enough. Could somebody die falling from a two-story window? I have no choice—I have to chance it.

I toss out my backpack, and it lands on the grass. Then I climb out the window, stand at the edge of the roof, and look down. The only sounds I hear are the voices in my head. I can see a green hose rolled up next to the house. And some empty flower pots from when Dad had decided to take up gardening that one time.

The largest tree branch is maybe three or four feet away. Though I've often thought about trying this, I never actually did because I was always too scared. It's too far—I won't make it. I could end up breaking my arm. Or worse. I could take the stairs, but I'm pretty sure Dad would hear me. The pain in my head from the voices is blinding me. I have to try. *Just do it, Ivan.*

Taking a breath, I crouch down, then spring forward. Amazingly, I catch the branch and hook both arms around it. Now, what? I look down. The lights are on in the den, which means Dad is watching TV. Using one arm at a time, I swing forward inch by inch till I am close enough to the base of the branch to get a foothold. Then I push myself toward the center of the tree and, steadying myself, stand straight up on the thickest part. Finally, I climb down to the lowest branch, jump off, and land on my butt on the wet grass.

I can hear Luckman yelling at his dog. He sounds drunker than usual. One time, I saw Dad go outside to see what was going on. When my neighbor spotted him, he threatened to shoot Dad if he didn't mind his own damn business. Dad had had a few beers and wasn't scared at all. He took out his cell phone to call 911. Grinning, Luckman picked up the dog by the scruff of the neck and carried him back into the house.

I sneak around the side of the house now, silently unlatch the gate, and run to the sidewalk. I would've taken my skateboard, but I was afraid the wheels would make too much noise. I race along the grass till I'm way past my house. Then I continue on to the gas station. As I get closer, I see the flashing lights and hear the familiar sound of a police radio.

Two cop cars are sitting nose-to-nose in the parking lot with their lights on. A fire truck and an ambulance are parked next to them. And some gangbangers are sitting on the curb in handcuffs. I move a little closer. That's when I see the body. One of the EMTs is already zipping up the body bag. The concrete is covered in fresh blood. One of the cops is placing a severed hand in an evidence bag.

So much for Plan A. I decide to head to the school.

I HAD NEVER BEEN at the school this late at night. The place is creepy and deserted—not even a janitor around. Far away, someone is screaming. Or is that in my head? I've heard the cops sometimes patrol the area, looking for vandals. I'll have to be quick. I run over to where the old lockers are and enter through the gate. The voices are angry now.

The door to Craig's locker is ajar like it always is. My heart racing, I set down my backpack and remove the contents one by one. Lighter fluid, matches, and the notebook. Opening the locker door, I place the notebook inside. I hear a noise and look around. Nothing. The voices have stopped, but my head still hurts. I keep seeing images of my family in hell—flames everywhere—their arms raised like they're pleading with me. But I can't stop. It's almost done.

I pop open the top of the can and squirt most of the lighter fluid onto the notebook, completely soaking it. The smell of butane gets up in my nose, making me a little high. I set the can down on the ground, take one of the kitchen matches, and light it. Before tossing it in, I remember to stand back to avoid getting burned. I'm about to toss the match in when I hear a gasp.

"No, don't!" a voice says.

It isn't one of the voices in my head, though. I turn around and see Hershey the janitor limping toward me. What is that old coot doing here at this hour? Ignoring him, I toss the match in, and a ball of flame shoots out of the locker, almost frying me. Hershey is next to me now, breathing hard. He grabs my hand.

"What in hell'd you do that for?" he says.

"I had to stop it."

"Stop it? Stupid kid. You didn't stop anything. Look!"

He's pointing inside the locker. Though the flames are

consuming the notebook, it isn't turning to ash the way I thought it would. Something greenish and bright is rising out of the smoke. It looks like...*claws*.

"What is it?"

"Get behind me, kid," he says.

Taking a greasy rag from his back pocket, he uses it to slam the locker shut. As quickly as he can, he spins the combination lock to keep the door from opening again. I can hear a piercing scream and pounding coming from the locker. It's unreal. Using one hand, Hershey takes off his shirt, balls it up, and presses it against the door to keep in whatever it is that's trying to escape.

"You know where the janitor's room is?" he says.

"Sure."

"Take the keys off my belt, go in there, and look for a can of red spray paint. Bring it back here. Quick! I can't hold this door closed forever!"

The janitor's room door is open. Inside, the can is sitting on a shelf all by itself. I grab it and rejoin Hershey. The thing inside the locker is going batshit. I pull off the top and hand the spray can to the janitor. He drops the shirt and sprays a bizarre symbol on the door. It's a circle with some writing around it. And in the middle are symbols I've never seen before.

"What is that?"

Hershey steps away, sets the can down on the ground, and puts his shirt back on. I realize the thing inside isn't making any noise.

"A sigil," he says.

"A what?"

"It's for warding off evil. Come on."

I stuff everything into my backpack, and we run toward the parking lot. The only car sitting out there is a metallic blue Ford Fairlane in perfect condition.

"Get in," he says, climbing in behind the wheel.

I'm scared of the old man, but he did save my life, so I climb in the passenger side and plop down on the cushy vinyl upholstery. As soon as I've buckled the old-fashioned seat belt, we peel out of there. My heart is still beating so fast; it takes me a while to notice the voices and the headache have completely stopped.

Hershey refuses to say anything on the way to his place. I always thought this guy was a loser and lived under a bridge somewhere. But as we walk in, I can see that the one-bedroom apartment is neat. I recognize Ikea furniture and lamps. And though the old man's appearance needs work, he keeps the place nice. I also notice there are no family photos anywhere—only religious statues.

I take a seat on the sofa as he heads into the kitchen. "Hershey, what was that thing?"

"My name's James, by the way. Hershey's my last name."

"I'm Ivan."

"Want somethin' to drink?"

"No thanks. So, can you tell me what it was?"

"A demon," he says, taking a seat next to me and popping open a soda. "Actually, multiple demons."

"So, Craig was a demon?"

"No. He was a stupid kid who used to get picked on a lot."

"Like me and Ollie."

"Yeah. Finally, he got sick of it, so he... I told him to stay away from that Satanist."

"What's a Satanist?"

"Somebody who communes with demons."

"You mean, there's some guy running around putting people in touch with, with...the Devil?"

"*Demons.* He used to live in this town. Went by the

name o' Bob Raven. His house was over on Rhodo-
dendron."

"Isn't that by the mall?"

"Wasn't a mall back then. The neighborhood was all
houses with a couple o' schools. City condemned the whole
thing when some big developer came in and offered them
millions to build a brand-new shopping center. Raven's
house was part o' the deal."

He goes over to a small desk and opens a drawer. Pulls
out what looks like a scrapbook. When he sits down, he
hands it to me. As I flip through, I see pages of old newspaper clippings with photos. One of them is of a white-
haired old man dressed in black and wearing a black hat,
standing at a podium. He looks like an undertaker. The
caption reads, CITIZEN TESTIFIES AT PUBLIC ZONING
HEARING.

"That's Bob Raven," he says.

"So, they were going to kick him out of his house?"

The janitor nods. "And no matter what he did, he
couldn't fight it. But he tried. Lord, he tried. That was a
bad year, Ivan. Two council members dead from freak
accidents. Kids gone missing. A whole lotta mutilated pets.
The worst of it was on Halloween. All o' the houses on one
street burned right to the ground. Some people said it was
Bob Raven, but they could never prove anything."

"So, what happened?"

He takes a long swallow and looks at me. "There's no
way you can scare a crooked politician—that's a fact. And
the mayor was as crooked as they come. The deal went
through all right. The mayor and his buddies got paid off,
and Raven was forced out. The mayor must've feared
Raven, though. Because after they tore down his house, he
called in an expert from some Christian college to salt the
ground."

"Why?"

"To purify it."

The old man explains to me how, while all this was going on, Craig had heard about Bob Raven and decided to visit him. He was a seventh grader at the time—like me. One day he rode his old bike over and gave Raven all of the money he'd been saving for a new one—three hundred bucks. Raven promised to coach him after school. Craig went over there every day.

The Satanist never gave the kid anything in writing. Instead, he made him copy stuff down in the notebook. Then he performed a ritual over it. When he was finished, Raven told the kid to go through the list and recite the spells and all of his troubles would be over.

"So, Craig made the list from Bob Raven's instructions?"

"He did indeed," James says. "I kept telling him to stop, but he wouldn't. In fact, he became even more determined. Turns out the list was the curse ol' Bob Raven had put on the town."

"Whatever happened to him?"

"No one knows."

"And Craig?"

The old man looks away. I can see he's crying, but I pretend not to notice.

"James?"

"We lost a lot of people that year. Some who'd never done anything to hurt Craig. Some who had."

"And Craig made it through the whole list?"

"Yeah. Then he disappeared. Like Bob Raven." He wipes his eyes on his sleeve. "The thing is, Raven knew all along what would happen to Craig if he made it through the list."

I think about what Ollie had told me. Craig was in hell,

along with the rest of the demons probably. Something occurs to me.

"Hey, James. How come you know all this stuff about Craig?"

He gives me a sad look and smiles, holes showing where normal teeth should be.

"He was my best friend."

"What? When did all this happen?"

"1967. Craig and I went to school together."

"Holy shit! But if you knew, why didn't you destroy the notebook yourself?"

He's angry now, and I'm wondering if it had been a mistake coming home with him.

"The notebook vanished with Craig. After that, I thought everything was fine. I graduated high school and went to work as a mechanic. Seven years later, I read about some kids in the area who'd died mysteriously. On a hunch, I went over to the school to check things out. That's when I found Craig's old locker. And the notebook inside."

"Why did it come back?"

"I don't know, but it was seven years to the day Craig disappeared."

"Did you try to get rid of it then?"

"Sure, but it wouldn't let me near it. It was like there was this force around it, protecting it. I knew it was a matter o' time before some other bullied kid found it, so I quit my job and went to work as a janitor at the school. I needed to keep kids away from the evil. That's what I've been doing all these years."

I feel like someone gut-punched me. "James, I am so sorry. I mean for everything. And about treating you like…"

"It's okay, Ivan. I'm used to it."

He gets to his feet and throws away the soda can. I'm

thinking about Craig and about what I did to Franklin. James must know what I'm thinking because now he's standing in front of me, looking serious.

"How far did you get?" he says.

I don't want to talk about this, and I stand up to leave. He grabs my arm; he looks angry. I try to pull away.

"How far?"

"Almost to the end."

"So, you didn't do the last step?"

"No."

"But it was you who killed that kid in the skate park."

I'm scared he's going to call the cops on me. "No, I—"

"Don't lie to me, boy. You killed him using demon power."

I'm shaking now. "He killed my friend! I—I didn't mean to do it, I swear! It just happened. I tried to stop, but—"

He lets go and pats my shoulder. "Shh…"

"Are you going to tell the cops?"

He looks at me and shakes his head. "They'd think I was crazy. How could a kid rip somebody's head off?"

"James, your eyes!"

Blood is running down from his eyes like tears. Unafraid, he walks into the bathroom and rinses his face. When he returns, he looks normal again.

"That's been happening ever since I returned to the school," he says.

"Does it hurt?"

"No."

"Jeez, James, you really scared me. What are we going to do about the notebook?"

"I don't know, kid. You can't destroy it with fire. Or anything else. The sigil you saw me draw? I painted that thing on the door lots o' times, but rust keeps eating it away. Usually takes about two or three days." He stands. "Let's get you home. Your folks must be worried."

I walk outside and wait for the old man to grab his keys. There's someone in the parking lot, standing alone in the dark. A man dressed in black and wearing a hat. He looks ancient, with pale skin, black eyes, and long white hair. He's looking right at me. My blood turns to ice.

It's Bob Raven.

WE'RE SITTING outside my house in the car. All of the lights are off, and everyone's in bed. I'd decided not to tell James about what I saw earlier.

"Can I ask you a question?"

"Sure," he says.

"The list calls for a sacrifice. For me, it was my friend Ollie. I don't mean to be disrespectful, but…"

"Why ain't I dead? Because Craig had no problem cutting off his finger like the list called for. He wanted the power so bad, and he didn't care what he had to do. None of the bad stuff ever touched me. I guess that's the one thing I can be grateful for."

"Sorry."

For the first time, I notice he's wearing a gold cross around his neck. It looks too small for him, like it was made for a kid. He catches me looking at it and holds it.

"Got this when I made my First Communion," he says. "I was eight. It's blessed."

"So, are you religious?"

"My parents raised me Catholic. Never used to believe in any o' that stuff the priest told us. But it's real, Ivan. Don't let anyone ever tell you different. It's why I pray all the time."

"Sometimes I wish I could pray. You know, for my family and stuff."

"Just do it. It ain't hard."

I run across the lawn to the back gate. Then I go inside, climb the tree, and hop over to my bedroom window. It's almost twelve-thirty. Everyone is asleep. I try doing the same, but there's too much going on in my head. Demons are living inside Craig's old locker. Sooner or later, the door will open and they'll escape. What then? A worse thought hits me.

When they do get free, I'll be the first on their list.

NOW THAT OLLIE'S DEAD, I have no reason to be late for school. I don't blame him, you understand. We would take our time, talking all the way there—I can't even remember about what. Though we had just seen each other the day before, we always had something new to say. As I head over to the campus on my skateboard, flying solo, I still talk to him, but only in my head. Lame, right?

When I arrive at school, Kirk is waiting for me. Alone. He looks like Jason minus the hockey mask, ready to kill somebody. Me. I pretend to ignore him and skate past. He just stands there, watching me. I'm surprised when he doesn't do anything, and I keep going.

I take my books from my locker. The warning bell hasn't rung yet. When I turn around, Kirk is standing there again, that same evil look on his face. Those tools he likes to hang out with are behind him, grinning. Closing my eyes and taking a breath, I prepare for the beating of my life. Other kids are standing around us as if someone had sent out a secret invitation to a fight. I clear my throat and look at Kirk.

"What?"

"How'd you know about my parents?" he says.

I have to think fast. The voices are no longer in my head to help me, and I can't see anything new about Kirk's life. He's like any other stranger—a mystery. *Think, Ivan!*

"Kirk, *everyone* in school knows."

I glare at his two friends. Then Kirk does the same, his anger building. Too stupid to know what just happened, his buddies look at each other. Then one of them catches on, and his little rat's eyes become huge.

"We didn't say nothin', Kirk! I swear!"

Screaming like a wounded animal, Kirk grabs each of them by the collar and smashes their heads together, which makes a dull thud like watermelons hitting the ground. Then he drives them into the lockers as the crowd chants.

"Fight! Fight! Fight!"

I slip away before Mr. Charbonneau and the other teachers arrive and head around back by the chain link fence. When I pass Craig's locker, I notice that the sigil is lighter and rust is eating away at the edges. Unable to resist, I go inside and touch the door with my finger. It's hot, yet there isn't any smoke. The warning bell rings, and I have to run all the way to class. I have a feeling I won't be seeing Kirk for a long time.

At lunch, I find James sitting inside the janitor's room with the door open. He's holding a bologna sandwich in one hand and a juice box in the other. But he's staring at the ground like he doesn't even know the food is there.

"James?"

He looks up. His eyes seem hollow and dark. I can see a dried drop of blood on his cheek. He tries to smile, but it comes off as fake.

"You okay, Ivan?"

"Yeah. The locker—"

"I know. The demons are still inside. It's gonna come open. Matter o' time."

"What can we do? How about calling a priest?"

"I don't think so."

"Then what?"

"I shoulda stopped him," he says.

"Who?"

"Craig. This is my fault. I coulda done it if I'd tried harder."

I feel bad for the old man. After all these years, he still carries the guilt of losing his best friend. But it's not his fault, the way it wasn't my fault that Ollie died. I don't know what to say.

"I'm gonna fix this," he says. "Tonight."

I'm worried about him. I don't know when it happened, but I've come to care about the old man. From what I can see, he hasn't had much of a life. He doesn't deserve this.

"James, what are you talking about?"

He throws his lunch in the trash and gives me a pat on the head. "Go on, now. Take care o' yourself. And don't ever mess with Satanists or Ouija boards or nothin'. You hear what I'm tellin' you, Ivan?"

"Sure, James, but—"

"Leave!" he says. "Ain't you got class? Go on."

He scowls at me as if he hates everything about me, so I take off, cursing him under my breath. That's what I get for caring about some stupid old man. He can rot in hell, for all I care. Maybe it's what he wants—to join his friend down there.

———

IT'S NIGHT, and I'm sitting in my room, trying to do homework. But I can't concentrate. The headaches and the voices haven't returned, but all I can think about is what James said. *I'm gonna fix this.* I can't imagine what he could even do. If he opens the locker, the evil will escape. Then what? I use my computer to do a quick search on demons. So much has been written about them—demons, demonology, *demonic possession*… Then it hits me. I need to go to the school right away. Maybe it isn't too late.

It's only been dark half an hour. My dad and Beth are out. I convince Mom I have to run down the street to a friend's house to pick up some homework I forgot about. I promise to be back soon. She buys it.

Outside, as I pass Luckman's house, I hear something. It sounds like talking. Though I'm in a hurry, I decide to take a quick look. I sneak up to the fence and peer through the crack by the gate. Luckman is standing in the dark, next to a big oak tree. His dog is next to him, whining softly. One of those Coleman battery lanterns sits on the ground, bathing the scene in a white glow that makes my neighbor look like a sad ghost.

Luckman takes another swallow from the bottle he's holding and looks at the dog. I'm afraid he's going to punish the animal again, but he just stares at it. Then he sets the bottle down, crouches, and strokes the animal's fur. I must've coughed because my neighbor turns around. I back away and make my way silently to the sidewalk.

I run all the way to the school, hoping I'm not too late. When I arrive, I see James' car in the parking lot. Maybe there's still time. I hurry to where the old lockers are and find the janitor standing in front of Craig's locker, spray paint in one hand—tan paint, the same color as the locker door.

"James!"

He looks at me as I approach, his eyes angry and sad at the same time.

"I told you to stay away, Ivan."

"Don't do it, James. Please. We'll find another way."

"There ain't no other way. This was always the answer. I knew it in my heart, but I refused to accept it. Please, go. I have to do this."

A horrible screeching noise echoes from inside the locker, and the sound of banging on metal starts up. I can see the locker door buckling from the force. Soon, it will burst open on its own. I can't think what to do to stop this.

"James, no!"

But he's not listening. Instead, he removes his cross and places it in my hands. Then, raising the spray can, he paints out the sigil as the screeching and pounding become louder. As he does this, his eyes begin bleeding again. I feel like my heart will explode, and I drift back. The pounding is hurting my ears as James throws away the can. Then the door flies open. A greenish glow lights up the old man, and his eyes bug out. The screeching dies down to a kind of purr and multiple greenish claws with black fingernails reach toward him.

I can see that James is afraid, but he doesn't move. Instead, he shuts his eyes and waits. A flash of green light shoots out, and James falls onto his knees. Holding his head, he roars with pain, as if those things inside him are eating him alive. Then he looks at me, his eyes no longer human. They're blood red, and they look like fire. He tries speaking, but he can only choke out a single word.

"Run!"

I don't want to leave the old man, but I know it's not him anymore. So, I do as he says. As I reach the sidewalk, I hear a car door slam and an engine starting. When I turn around, I can see James driving off, peeling out of the parking lot like a drag racer. He zooms out past me and onto the deserted street. Then he's gone.

THE STREETS ARE quiet as I make my way home. When I reach Luckman's house, I can see cop cars, a fire engine, and an ambulance. EMTs are rolling a gurney with a body bag on it toward the ambulance. Soon after, a cop exits the house, walking my neighbor's dog on a leash. Though I don't like talking to cops, I decide to find out what's going on and walk up to one of the detectives who interviewed me.

"You shouldn't be here," he says.

"What happened?"

"Suicide."

Another cop walks out of the house, carrying a shotgun in a clear plastic evidence bag. The cop with the dog stops next to us. I had never seen Luckman's dog up close before. He's old, and his back is covered in scars. He looks at me, one eye watering more than the other.

"What do we do with him?" the cop says to the detective.

I reach for the leash. "I want him."

"What about your parents?"

"They won't mind. Please."

The detective nods to the cop. Then to me, "See if you can give him a better life than Mr. Luckman did."

Mom is waiting for me at home with milk and cookies. She hadn't done that in years. When she sees the dog, she doesn't say anything. I take a seat at the kitchen table, and the dog lies down next to me.

"He was so alone," she says, patting the dog's head. "What's his name?"

"I'm naming him Ollie."

She kisses me on the head. "Good. Ollie it is, then."

Now the hot tears come. Tears for Ollie and James and all the other people in this town who've ever suffered. I don't have it so bad. Mom stands behind me, holding me and making soothing noises. I suddenly feel very tired. Mom notices and touches my face.

"Why don't you go to bed?" she says. "I'll clear a nice spot for Ollie, and tomorrow, we'll buy him some food. Okay, Ivan?"

But I don't say anything.

WHEN I COME DOWNSTAIRS in the morning, my dog greets me, wagging his tail. I find Dad sitting at the kitchen table, wearing a suit. He's shaven, and his hair is cut. Beth is finishing up some homework, and Mom's making breakfast for everyone—eggs, bacon, the works. Normally, I would beat it out of the house without eating. Today, I decide I need to be with my family. I'm wearing James' cross under my shirt. I still don't know if I believe in God, but after everything that's happened, I feel like it will protect me, the way it protected James all those years.

"Shame what happened to Luckman," Dad says. "Ivan, you did a good thing volunteering to take his dog." He scratches the animal behind his ear.

"Did you notice your father's wearing a suit?" Mom says to me.

"Yeah, what gives?"

Dad smiles and messes up my hair, which he knows I hate. "I have a job interview, Ivan."

"Way to go, Dad!"

A newscaster's voice interrupts us. I see Mom adjusting the small portable TV sitting on the kitchen counter.

"In other news, a local man lost control of his car last night on a mountain road, plunging eight hundred feet into a ravine. A witness who was directly behind the vehicle called 911. Emergency crews arrived within minutes. A helicopter was used to lower rescuers into the ravine.

"No one other than the driver was in the vehicle at the time of the accident. He was pronounced dead at the scene. Police have identified him as James Hershey, a janitor at a local middle school. It is believed Mr. Hershey has no immediate family. Next up, traffic."

Mom turns off the TV and shakes her head. "That poor man. Did you know him, Ivan?"

"Not really."

"He must've been drinking," Dad says. "Why else would he drive off a cliff?"

After breakfast, I grab my skateboard and head for school. I think about Kirk. He'd been suspended for fighting, but I know sooner or later he'll return. I don't care. I realize I don't hate him the way I thought I did. Hey, I'm not insane. I know we'll never be friends or anything, but maybe we can at least live and let live. One day at a time, I guess.

At school, two men in dark blue coveralls are ripping out all the old lockers. I watch as they drill out the bolts and yank the lockers out one by one. And for a second, I think I see James standing behind the men. My imagination probably.

I mean, seriously. Whoever heard of a ghost making an appearance during the day?

Nailed It

THE FLIGHT HAD ALREADY BEEN DELAYED FORTY-THREE minutes. Jerry tapped out a few more sentences on his laptop and considered what he'd written.

"What's that, a book?"

The closeness of the voice made Jerry look over. He acknowledged the kid sitting by the window, an empty seat separating them. He was in his early twenties, with gray teeth. Gaunt and pale like a survivor from the dead of a Detroit winter.

He was typically dressed—blue jeans torn precisely at the knees, a faded tee shirt from some long-forgotten rock concert, and a new silver-studded black leather jacket. His short, spiky hair, gauged earlobes, and nervous look made Jerry curious.

"It's a story," Jerry said. He cringed as he waited for the inevitable follow-up.

"What's it about?" At least the kid seemed sincere.

"Well, it's really about compulsion. You know, compulsive behavior."

"Oh, yeah."

He did not understand in the least. Instead, he read the warning on the emergency exit next to him. An apologetic flight attendant appeared. Her pleasantness developed a momentary chink, manifesting itself as a pronounced facial tic as her eyes quickly took in the kid, then happily migrated toward Jerry.

"Are you both prepared to assist in case of an emergency?"

"Yes," Jerry said.

Not making eye contact, the kid nodded. "Sure."

"The captain is so sorry about the delay. We're going to serve some snacks now."

"How much longer, do you think?" Jerry said.

"I don't know. It's hard to say with all this fog. Maybe twenty minutes?"

"Mm."

"Would you like beer or wine?"

Jerry said "Mm" again as the flight attendant distributed little foil bags of sweet salted nuts and cheddar cheese Goldfish. Soon after, complimentary wine and beer followed. Jerry decided on a glass of some generic merlot.

"Free beer, that's pretty awesome," the kid said. "I hate flying, except for the free beer."

"Mm."

Jerry tried losing himself in his writing. Strangely, something about this kid reminded him of the man in the story. Peripherally, he watched as his tightly wound companion examined each of the four foil bags, took a swallow of beer, and started at the beginning.

"I knew a guy once—" Jerry said.

"What!" The kid seemed startled and almost spilled his beer.

"Sorry. I was just saying, I knew a guy once who was

neat to the point of neurosis. I guess you laying out those little bags reminded me of him."

"Oh."

As the skittery kid feigned attention, his hands deliberately disarranged the bags on the tray table. He craned his neck, looking for the flight attendant, hoping maybe he could switch seats with someone before they took off.

"Anyway," Jerry said, "this guy was the nicest person you'd ever want to meet. Loved his wife, kind to animals. All that. But he was agitated a lot of the time. Something ate at him, and nobody could figure out what it was. He seemed to want to *do* something."

"Like what?"

The kid was now making alternating rows of nuts and Goldfish. He was careful to make the Goldfish all point in the same direction. Any damaged items were quickly consumed.

"Well, he never said. But it kind of had to do with his job. You know, his life. I guess you could say he was dissatisfied. He'd always been a middle achiever. Average grades in school, average athletic skills, average dreams."

"So, an American."

Jerry chuckled. "Yeah, but this kind of thing had been going on for years. The middle job, the middle house in the housing tract."

"Was his wife average, too?"

"Actually, she was very sweet. And pretty. High school graduate, though."

"There you go."

"But the one thing this guy—let's call him 'Willie'—the one thing Willie excelled at was neatness. He was a neat freak. Once a week, he rearranged his furniture, attempting in a limited feng shui kind of way to copy the rooms he'd seen in *Architectural Digest*.

"His garage was a shrine to orderliness right down to the last little jelly jar of wood screws. His car was immaculate, too. He had had the seats covered in clear plastic."

"I hate wood screws," the kid said.

Jerry told him all about Willie, his meager hopes and dreams, his fears. He talked about Willie's father who died under mysterious circumstances at the age of forty-three. And about his mother who had dominated both their lives to an unhealthy degree.

The flight attendant brought more merlot and beer. Then Jerry got to the part where he was invited over to Willie's house for dinner.

"Willie wanted everything to be perfect. He refused to let his wife go to the grocery store and went himself. Even cooked the meal. He cleaned the house, washed the windows, and lit a fire.

"Everything was nearly picture perfect. Except the dog kept slinking away from the fireplace. I guess it was too hot for her."

"How was the chow?"

"Terrible. Poor Willie couldn't cook to save his life. But we all made nice and told him how wonderful it all was. I think he knew better. After that night, I didn't see him for a long time. I was doing a lot of traveling back then. We sort of lost touch.

"Then one day, I got an invitation in the mail. It was from Willie. He wanted to have me over for dinner. He promised it would be flawless this time, and practically ordered me to come.

"Part of me wanted to, but I had to teach a seminar that weekend. So I sent an email thanking him and promising to take his wife and him out to dinner sometime soon."

"Did he, like, freak out?"

"No. He sent me a very nice card to say that he and his wife were very much looking forward to dinner. The weird thing is, the note was written in that old-style calligraphy. You know, like they do on awards certificates? I didn't even know Willie could draw."

"Maybe his wife did it, or some art school dude."

"The last night of my seminar, I got home very late—after eleven. There were five messages on my machine, all from Willie.

"Each one sounded more...disturbed than the last. Something about having to see me urgently. I was about to erase the messages when the phone rang. I knew it was Willie."

"Oooooo-eeeeee-oooooooo!" the kid said, waggling his fingers.

"He was so relieved I was home and pleaded with me to come over for just a minute. All I wanted was to go to bed, but he sounded so, I don't know, *helpless*. So I decided to go."

Jerry paused and finished off his wine. The plane was taxiing down the runway now, getting in line for takeoff. The flight attendant took their trash and secured the tray tables. Jerry slipped his laptop under the seat.

He rubbed his eyes and shuddered a little, remembering that awful night and what he found when he went into the house. One of the flight attendants was pantomiming the safety procedures as another delivered her over-rehearsed amplified monolog.

"Please take a moment to find the emergency exit nearest you," the PA voice said. The kid tentatively probed the clear plastic cover over the red exit door handle.

Jerry braced himself. "When I got there, Willie answered the door, wearing a tuxedo. He was gibbering cheerfully about achievement of excellence or something and explaining that he'd finally managed to bring some kind of order to his life and just wanted me to see for myself so I wouldn't think he was crazy.

"I stepped into the house, and the first thing I smelled was Glade air freshener. Only it seemed like he had dumped a gallon of it into the air conditioning.

"The walls and ceilings had been freshly painted. There was new tile on the floor. I could see a warm fire in the living room. The dog was lying peacefully in front of it.

"Willie kept giggling like a lunatic as he took me on a tour of the kitchen, den, and finally, the living room. What I saw in there made me want to scream.

"The room actually sparkled. All of the old furniture had been replaced by new modern pieces. The stereo played quietly in the background—a Mozart string quartet, I think. Track lighting created these dramatic shadows. And expensive black-and-white photographs hung on the whitewashed walls.

"Willie's wife sat at one end of the sofa. She was wearing an elegant black evening dress and black satin pumps. One arm rested on the armrest. The other lay on her thigh, as if she were in repose. Her eyes begged me to stop this.

"'It's perfect,' Willie said. 'Isn't it perfect?' As I came closer, I could see that both her arms had been lashed into place with very thin copper wire that was cutting into her skin.

"She kept making these little groaning noises. I realized she couldn't open her mouth. It was as if it had been glued shut with epoxy. Then, I looked at her feet. They had been nailed to the floor. The blood didn't seem to bother Willie.

"'Don't worry,' he said. 'I gave her a local.'"

THEY WERE in the air now, climbing to cruising altitude. Jerry ordered another drink, pulled out his laptop, and went back to work.

The nervous kid stared out the window as objects on the ground became a soft, receding blur. As they gained altitude, the orderliness of the houses and the lawns and the streets seemed to please him, and he removed the protective plastic cover on the exit door.

He wanted a closer look.

Brown the Recluse

THURSDAY. BROWN RETURNED HOME FROM THE FUNERAL exhausted and discovered his key no longer fit the lock. Thunder boomed outside as he tried jiggling the damned thing, pulling on the door and cursing. Frustrated, he trudged back down the overlit hallway to the elevator and hit the down button. He hoped the apartment manager was in.

"Welcome back," the moon-faced man said through teeth too big for his face. He reeked of lemon oil and wore a nameplate with the name "Wayne" on it.

"My key doesn't work."

"Yes, we've had to change everyone's lock," Wayne said in a voice that suggested some kind of cosmic good fortune. Brown longed for the old manager. "Didn't you get the memo?"

"Isn't it obvious, if I had gotten the memo—" He decided not to pursue it. Anyway, this guy was deranged. "Can you just tell me what happened?"

"It's all in the memo," Wayne said. His voice was too

loud. Did the idiot think Brown was deaf? "Wait, I'll get it for you."

He stepped away and, returning with a plain white envelope, presented it. As the manager watched, Brown unsealed it. Inside, he saw a shiny brass key and the memo. When he turned to leave, Wayne said, "I'll need the other key."

Irritated, Brown pried the key off his old scratched key ring and handed it over. Leaving the envelope and the memo on the desk, he thanked the hapless moron and returned to his apartment.

As he entered carrying his bag, the first thing he noticed was how nothing whatsoever had changed. The apartment smelled musty. Outside, a hard rain was coming down. Fractured light fell like broken glass through curtains that were tan and immutable. Modest cloth furniture recoiled to the touch and stacks of books pleaded to be left alone. Brown didn't mind any of it. He went into the kitchen and poured himself a glass of wine. Then, he checked the answering machine and noted the glowing green zero. As he turned away, he saw something skitter across the floor.

He was certain it was a spider.

To the best of his knowledge, Brown had never seen a spider in his apartment. His heart raced. He closed his eyes tightly and tried to picture the vicious thing in his mind. It was medium-sized, its body the size of a dime. And it was sort of a tannish brown. Was that bad? How could it have gotten in? He never opened the windows, not even in summer.

He walked over to the laptop and, sitting at a small black-brown desk, searched the Internet. It didn't take long for him to find a vivid color photo of a brown recluse spider. Next, pictures of morbid bite wounds. His stomach did a somersault, and he felt a rush of heat.

Brown couldn't think. He checked the windows in the kitchen and living room. All closed. Feeling ill suddenly, he hurried to the bathroom. The little he had eaten came up in one lurching thrust that sent a spray of acid water past his teeth and over his dry lips. Weak, he flushed the toilet, found his way to the sink, and drenched his face in cold water. As he dried himself with a fresh hand towel, he stared into the mirror and gasped at the reflection of the small window above the shower.

It was open!

The phone conversation with the apartment manager was neither pleasant nor coherent. Between cascades of crushing stomach cramps, Brown said he *never* left the windows open. Wayne insisted otherwise. No one had opened any windows—they had simply changed the front door lock —and also, he would greatly appreciate it if Brown didn't yell at him. It was hopeless. Grabbing his stomach, he hung up.

Clutching a flashlight, he carefully worked his way around the kitchen on his hands and knees. The brown recluse was also known as the violin spider, after the pattern on its back. If threatened, it would normally run away. And it usually only bit when tangled up in clothing or bedding. The resulting wound was painful but rarely fatal.

Later when the phone rang, Brown thought about not answering, but it might have been the Chinese takeout driver lost again.

"Hello?"

"Are you okay, Dad?" It was his daughter in San Diego. She had driven him to the airport earlier. Was that today?

"I'm fine."

"I'm so glad you came." Her voice was the tremolo he recognized from when she was a little girl.

He wanted to comfort her but didn't know how. Women's emotions were a mystery to him, and he wished he never had to deal with them. "I think your mother would have liked it."

"I'm sorry you couldn't stay longer," Grace said. "We had the guest bedroom made up." He detected a hint of accusation.

"Me, too. I couldn't make it work."

"I understand. Thanks for coming down, though."

"Give the kids a kiss for me." He always used that phrase, because he could never remember their names. He barely knew his daughter's name. At Christmas, he sent them gift cards addressed to Grace.

"I will." This last response was followed by the long, painful silence of impossible distance.

"Bye, Dad."

"Bye."

After he had hung up, Brown realized he couldn't think of the reason he had gone to the funeral in the first place. Work was piling up and, though it was only a two-hour flight, getting through airport security was a pain in the ass. He and his ex-wife—Mary?—had been divorced for fifteen years. When he heard about her death, he had only a dim recollection of a middle-aged woman crying at the kitchen table in their old house as he lectured her sharply, a drink in one hand. He must've gone because of their daughter.

The Chinese food was worse than usual. The only reason he didn't switch restaurants was that they had been certified as never adding MSG. Maybe that was the problem. And they were close, which meant he could get his food quickly. Unless the driver got lost, which happened frequently.

Brown had been unable to find any trace of the spider. It was after midnight by the time he had put away the packaged food and pots and pans in the kitchen, and the clothes, extra bedding, and boxes in his bedroom closet. Before going to bed, he changed the sheets and shook out the duvet outside in the hallway.

The brown recluse preferred to stay hidden. Brown had heard stories of families who had lived for long periods with the spiders without ever having been bitten. The thought sickened him. He read for a while in bed and, when that didn't distract him, he turned out the light, hoping that through some miracle he would be spared.

———————

FRIDAY. It was pitch black and pouring rain when the alarm went off at five-thirty. Brown crawled out of bed feeling weak and dizzy. Sleep had eluded him and, when he finally did doze off sometime after four, he dreamed of his children. They were young and happy, playing and singing a hymn in a black pit alive with spiders. He was younger too. When he reached into the pit to rescue them, they shrieked, with swollen red eyes and ugly fangs, and they went on singing. Then, morning came. But the strangest thing about the dream was, there had been more than one girl, whereas in real life, Grace was an only child.

Coughing up phlegm, he examined himself in the bathroom mirror and discovered a dark reddish swelling on his neck. He ran the hot water, soaked a washcloth, and applied it to the wound. His head in his hands, he sat on the toilet, moaning softly. "Shit!" he said, more afraid than he'd ever been.

Brown left the garage and, as he pulled into traffic, he

noticed the low apartment building next door covered in a blue-and-white plastic tent—something out of a circus for dead people. He imagined thousands of brown recluse spiders driven out by the poison and fleeing into his building. And he was convinced that son of a bitch Wayne *had* left the bathroom window open, hoping something ungodly would crawl through.

Now he directed his loathing at the apartment owner who had ordered the fumigation and wished he could torture him. He imagined sinking giant meat hooks into his back and ripping away chunks of flesh and lung as the man begged for mercy. He wondered where a person could even buy meat hooks.

As Brown examined the bite on his neck in the rearview mirror, someone blasted their horn. He realized he'd been sitting at the green light for who knew how long. Waving apologetically, he hit the gas and continued on in the dense rain. His neck was throbbing. He wondered how long before he could take something again for the pain.

"You can get dressed," the physician's assistant said as she disposed of the needle and syringe. "At least you won't get tetanus. You say you're taking Ibuprofen?"

"Yes…" She looked foreign, and Brown worried she might be a terrorist.

"That's fine. I'm also going to prescribe an antibiotic, to be safe. And you can take Benadryl for the swelling if you want."

He had buttoned his sleeves but waited to tuck in his shirt. The woman was at the door when she stopped and turned. He was afraid she might threaten him.

"Keep an eye on the lesion," she said. "If it doesn't start closing up in a day or two, I want to see you again."

"Sure."

He was positive he would never again go to urgent

care. When he was alone, it occurred to him he neither remembered the woman's name nor what she looked like. Was forgetfulness one of the symptoms?

As usual, Brown ate lunch at his desk. A *Wall Street Journal* lay untouched next to his half-eaten sandwich. He thought about his apartment and got angry all over again. The idea of fumigation made his chest tighten. He could almost smell the pungent gas. If he did allow them in to treat the apartment, the stench would never leave—he was certain of it. The poison would scar his lungs, and he would eventually die of COPD.

"I've got the marketing brief for you," a voice said.

Slowly, he raised his head and saw the hopeful, familiar face of a young woman whose name escaped him. She was a MBA intern who had been doing outstanding work for two or three months. She was especially adept at Microsoft Excel. He seemed to recall writing her a glowing recommendation.

"Are you okay?" she said.

"Just leave it. I'll take a look at it after lunch."

"Right." At the door, she turned to him. He thought he heard her say, "I hope everything is…"

She couldn't have been more than twenty-five. It was starting to come back to him. She had attended UW and had gotten her MBA from Pepperdine University in California. She was originally from Colorado. Her father was in commercial real estate. What the hell was her name?

In the men's room, Brown preferred to urinate alone, so he always went into a stall—usually the large handicapped one farthest away from the urinals. As he finished, he heard someone walk in talking urgently on a cell phone. He recognized the voice. It was…*the analyst*. Come on. He had worked with this guy for three years. They did a presentation together to the CMO last month. Or was it last spring? What was happening to his mind?

From the sound of the conversation, he guessed the man was having some kind of family crisis. One of his kids? Did he even have children? He tried not to listen, but the analyst was speaking loudly, and his voice echoed. Then, it was quiet. He thought the man must have been urinating.

Brown bolted from the stall and washed his hands. He wanted to get away before the analyst could finish. But he wasn't fast enough. He noticed the wound on his neck had turned brown, the skin around it granulated—almost necrotic. He was sure he would need to see another damned doctor soon.

"How are you?" the analyst said. His voice sounded like a bad connection.

"Fine."

"You don't look so good. Hey, is that a bug bite?"

"There's a spider in my apartment."

"Ooh, I hate spiders. Why don't you call the exterminator?"

"Can't. Allergic to the chemicals."

As he dried his hands, he could feel the ghostlike analyst observing him with suspicion bordering on schadenfreude. Apparently, he had completely forgotten about his own problems.

"Guess you'll have to smash it with your shoe." The analyst's tone was buoyant.

"Yeah." He pretended to chuckle and strode quickly to the door.

"Hey, what kind was it?" Brown feigned incomprehension. "The spider."

"I didn't get a good look," he said and slipped out.

As he made his way back to his office, Brown imagined

continuing on to the elevators, taking one down to the lobby, crossing the polished marble floor past the guard station to the parking garage elevators, descending to P2, speeding out of the garage and into traffic toward the floating bridge, cutting into the far right lane, and rocketing over the side into the icy gray-green waters of Lake Washington. The vision was serenely satisfying and filled him with a vague, familiar longing.

When they performed the autopsy, they would conclude the spider's poison had done something to his brain. The whole thing would be ruled an accident—not suicide. Grace, the sole beneficiary of his estate, would come out all right. She could use the money for the kids' college.

He had been standing by the elevators for some time. No one said anything as they passed. He took out his cell phone and pretended to text someone. He was surprised to see a message from Grace. *Love u*, it read. He replied with *:)*. He thought she might like it. Who knew what women liked?

That evening, Chao arrived late again. He could never recall where exactly the old man lived and usually ended up driving the wrong way to the other end of town where the stewbums liked to hang out. As he rang the buzzer, he heard a skittering noise inside. He listened for a moment and hit the buzzer again.

"Food's here!" he said in his command voice. Chao was born in the US and had no trace of an accent, though he spoke fluent Cantonese. "Hey!"

Eventually, the door opened. Inside, it was dark. The smell of dry leaves got up into Chao's nostrils, and his stomach tightened. Lately, the old man never seemed to come into the light. A pale disfigured hand with purplish-black veins reached out and snatched the brown paper bag.

The fingernails too were black, and the hairs on the back of the hand were thick and stiff like a wire brush. Whatever was inside, it didn't seem human.

Chao waited as the bag was set down on the floor. Fingers reappeared and, in a crazy sleight of hand, revealed a crisp twenty-dollar bill.

"Keep the change," a voice said in a parched whisper.

"Thanks." Chao hesitated. "You okay?" He had been bringing food to the old man for a long time and was genuinely concerned.

"Tired." The voice was small and far away—a muted trumpet.

"See you next time," Chao said, trying to sound upbeat.

The door closed, and the deliveryman found himself alone in a carpeted cave. He pocketed the cash and left.

"You notice he always orders the same thing?" Chao said to his grandmother later at the nearly empty two-star restaurant.

"Why you not tell him about the special?"

"Doesn't want to talk."

He tried to explain it to her in Cantonese. The old man was lonely and probably needed a friend. His grandmother warned him to stay away from strangers with black fingernails.

"I'm late every time, and he never complains," Chao said. "And he always leaves me a large tip."

"You don't get close to that old man," she said in English, her voice icy. "He maybe like boys."

"I don't think he likes anyone."

"Next time, tell him the special."

Later, Chao couldn't sleep. He kept seeing the deformed hand and hearing a discomfiting skittering in his head. Did the old man have a disease? He felt for the remote on the nightstand and switched on the TV, hoping to find something violent on cable.

———

MONDAY. The conference room was already mostly full when Brown walked in and took a seat toward the back. He had no idea what the meeting was about and watched curiously as the intern brought her laptop to the head of the table, connected it to the projector, and displayed a PowerPoint presentation—the one Brown had been working on.

"Since Mr. Brown couldn't be here today," she said, "I've been asked to show you where we are with the new campaign."

Had she actually said those words? He almost laughed out loud and looked at the others for confirmation that this was some kind of stupid prank. But they ignored him and remained focused on the familiar images he had approved the previous week.

Every so often someone would stop the intern to ask a question. "Did Ted sign off on the landing page?"

"Yes," she said. "We're open to suggestions, though."

"I don't see a 'Partner' tab on the website."

"We're waiting for the CMO to send us the final list of approved partners."

"I don't think slide twenty-nine is correct. Those look like last year's market share numbers."

"They are correct as of Q3."

Finally, the VP of Product Marketing asked the question Brown was dying to hear an answer to. "Why isn't Ted here?" he said.

Brown looked around the room, almost giddy at the thought this could be happening. He had been at the firm eleven years and had no enemies he knew of. Wait, what about that bastard, the analyst? No, what reason would he have? Any second, everyone would turn to him and say, "April Fools!" He had an impulse to jump onto the table and perform the tango from one end to the other. Or loudly break into "I Gotta Feeling" like a mental patient.

The silence was unnerving. The intern was visibly stressed, almost to the point of tears. He felt sorry for her.

"We can't find him," she said in a voice so soft he could barely hear.

"I see," the VP said. He glanced at his watch and looked around the room. "Let's continue."

"We intend to launch the site with this video case study on the landing page. Over the next twelve months, we will rotate in other videos."

Brown knew the video well. It was an interview with one of the principal researchers at a large pharmaceutical company that had implemented his company's flagship software product. But instead of the familiar talking head, he saw a silent security camera-quality image of himself standing near the elevators, pretending to text someone. No one but him thought this was out of order. They watched, rapt, as he put away his phone and purposefully walked off camera. Horizontal bars appeared across the video, making the image appear erratic. When it cleared, the analyst's head filled the screen, his face grinning hideously into the camera as he dangled a plastic spider on an elastic string.

Dizzy and nauseous, Brown got up awkwardly and slipped out of the room. No one seemed to care. Outside, it was cold. He had forgotten his overcoat and wandered up the street in the rain, oblivious to everything. By the time he reached Starbucks, he was drenched. Sucking back a sob, he slipped inside.

Warming his hands around a cup of black coffee, Brown sat in a chocolate brown leather chair and considered his options. He most certainly was *not dead*. This had to be a joke. And yet... He looked at his hands; they didn't belong to him. They looked like the hands of a strangler. He was suddenly very hungry.

It was after eight when Chao arrived in a steady rain. Having secured an excellent parking spot directly across from the manager's office, he felt lucky. As he approached the door entry system, he didn't see anyone in the office. He punched in the old man's extension and waited for the glass door to unlock. Tonight, Chao would talk to him, despite what his grandmother had said. It was the decent thing to do. This time he'd remembered the fortune cookies. He thought they would cheer up the old man.

"Food's here!" he said in the hallway.

The door opened slightly. Mixed with the smell of dry leaves came the odor of carrion. Chao wanted to vomit. He waited for the ghostly hand to appear. Nothing happened. As he tried sliding the bag through the opening, a rake-like claw took his arm. Something with extraordinary strength dragged him into the darkness inside and slammed the door shut.

Like a goat whose throat had been slit, a muffled voice bleated once. Then came crushing silence, except for the buzzing of a failing light bulb at the end of the hallway in an exit sign the residents had frequently complained about.

The rain had stopped.

WEDNESDAY. Brown crouched naked in the middle of the living room floor, watching the sunset through the windows. He could no longer stand. An engorged brownish sac protruded from his lower spine. His limbs were thin and brittle. Instead of fingers, he had two curved claws on each arm.

The bodies of Chao and others who had had the misfortune of knocking on his door were arranged in a circle around him, devoid of fluid—misshapen bags of bones and mortified tissue, the skin on each gray and leathery. Next to one lay a blood-spattered nameplate with the name "Wayne" on it.

Brown no longer thought about his daughter or work or any pleasure he had ever experienced in his former life. His only concern was to feed. He brightened when he realized the fumigators had finished with the apartment building next door. The tent had been removed, and people were coming and going freely. The windows were open, and he watched with pride as thousands of tiny spiders climbed the still curtains onto the hard ledge and poured out of the building.

THURSDAY. The incinerator in the basement roared to life as the maintenance man fed it old newspapers and piles of trash. A load of black garbage bags lay near the door. One by one he dragged them over, lifted each with a grunt, and tossed it in. One of the bags split open, and a decaying human arm fell out. Ignoring it, he gathered the bag together and tossed it into the fire.

Now he was staring at a gigantic dead spider lying on the cold concrete. A few wisps of gray hair were barely noticeable around the humanlike head. The eyes were black marbles, the smooth, dark mandibles caked with dried blood. He lifted the carcass easily, tossed it into the fire, and slammed the furnace door shut.

"Let's hope this is the last one," he said to no one and went off to enjoy a lunch of raw hamburger and beer.

Upstairs, Julie waited for the apartment manager to get off the phone. This was the part of the job she hated most —tracking down errant employees.

"Sorry about the wait," the young man said. His name was Steve, and he smelled like her ex-husband.

"We were worried and wanted to check on Mr. Brown," she said. "He hasn't been to the office for a long time, and we haven't heard from him. Have you seen him?"

Steve sat in front of the computer and keyed something in. "Which apartment?"

"SE 805."

After more typing, he brightened. "There was someone in the apartment. A Mr. Brown. But it's been unoccupied for weeks. We're having it cleaned soon, and we'll be putting it back on the market. Are you interested?"

"*Weeks?* What are you talking about? I want to see for myself."

The apartment smelled of earth and dry leaves. The late morning light streaming through the windows illuminated the scratches and other imperfections in the pale hardwood floor. The markings reminded Julie of insect tracks. Immediately, she crossed to the living room windows and stared down at the street.

Police cars, fire trucks, and ambulances surrounded the entrance of the neighboring apartment building. She counted seven black body bags lying in a row on the sidewalk. Two EMTs were bringing out another body on a gurney. She shivered as she turned back to the apartment manager.

"I can offer you a very attractive move-in package."

"I'm not looking for an apartment," she said impatiently as she inspected the other rooms. "I'm simply trying to determine what happened to this man."

"Brown. Yes, SE 805. He doesn't live here anymore."

She sighed deeply, grateful she no longer carried a hammer in her purse. As they left the apartment, she thought she felt something dance across her foot.

On the way back to the office, Julie tried to think how she would explain to the HR Director that an employee of their firm had simply vanished without a trace, leaving everything behind. As she pulled into the parking garage, she felt a sharp stab and saw something skitter under the passenger-side floor mat. It was brown. She looked at her ankle. A dark reddish swelling was beginning to form. Her heart swam up her throat.

"They don't pay me enough for this," she said, her voice like acid, and got out of the car to make her report.

I've Been Better

I'LL TELL YOU STRAIGHT HOW IT WAS—HOW I MET REESE and what that devil did to me—but you have to promise to listen to the whole thing. Okay? Relax. I'm buying.

I had a dream. It was after one of those late-night dinner meetings. First, there was the wine with dinner, then grappa after. Before I knew it, we were all in the hotel bar with Modelo and Porfidio Silver. Finally, just the añejo. I don't even remember how I got home. Anyway, the dream.

There are clouds—big, puffy ones, right? I can hear a squeaking noise like, like something needed grease. I turn around to see a huge pulley and a fat rope inching its way over. So, I look closer. Now I can see them—you know, the tips. They were silver.

Angel's wings.

I got Reese's number from a friend at work. We decide to try dinner. Reese insists we eat at a place I've never heard of called Totentanz in Brentwood. I remember it was cold and very windy. Guys in black vests are running around parking Bentleys, Maseratis, Teslas—you know the kind of place. Fashionably dressed-down people being blown into the restaurant like rich debris. The place stinks of money. I like it.

The valet who's got my car—his nameplate says "Stuart"—was a little disheveled, to be honest. Smelled kind of sour, too, like he hadn't bathed in a while. I guess they hire anybody. He looks me over real good and hands me my ticket.

"Try not to scratch it," I say. I always have to tell these schmucks; they don't respect other people's property.

Inside, it's nice. Huge reproductions of Bosch and Brueghel hang on the walls and also a few engravings I don't recognize. And here's the weird part. The restaurant —the whole place—is filled with nothing but couples, one at each table or booth. The lighting is really low. The waiters and the busboys are moving as quiet as ghosts. I see men and women, women and women, men and men. But the thing is, only one person at each table is doing the talking. Like speed dating, sort of. The other is sitting there listening intently. At one table, some guy is crying. I mean, he was actually *bawling*. What gives?

They lead me to a booth where Reese is already waiting. So, now we're drinking dirty martinis. Reese looks incredible by the way. Hey, I just noticed, you look a lot like Reese. So, I'm blabbing away, blabbing, drinking my martini, and Reese is hanging on my every word. I mean *every word*. I feel amazing. I don't know; maybe it was the alcohol.

"The thing of it is," I'm saying, "the account came to me by accident. You see, this guy Harlan had a triple bypass. He was supposed to come back to work after six weeks. All rested up. Well, he died instead."

I don't know why but I'm laughing like a hyena now.

You're not supposed to laugh when somebody dies, but I couldn't help it. It was funny.

Then Reese says, "How lucky are *you*?" There was a tone—I don't know, it's hard to describe.

"Hellz yeah!" I say. "I mean, I was broken up and all. But come on. What a break." So, I keep talking away. I tend to get loud when I drink, I'll admit. It's a shortcoming. Reese gives me a look, and I calm down immediately. It was like hypnotism or something.

"So, anyway," I say much quieter, "I totally reworked Harlan's old advertising campaign. Threw a modern angle on it. Added all the social media stuff. The old guy was past it. I'm surprised he lasted this long. I have to give a big presentation to the client tomorrow. I'm nervous as hell, I don't need to tell you."

"You'll do fine," Reese says. "I know you will."

Next thing I know, Reese has my hand. Nobody's ever… It freaked me out a little, if you want to know the truth.

"Yeah?" I say. "Well, so what? This kind of thing is right in my wheelhouse. No big deal."

"No big deal," Reese says.

The waiter shows up, and I realize that we've had dinner already. We've been there like three hours. The guy was the kind of server you fear, just saying. He doesn't talk to me; he talks to Reese. Come to think of it, I never even gave that guy my order. Reese did everything.

"Will there be anything else?" What a prick.

"No thanks, Salvador," Reese says.

Then, I jump in. "Could you bring the check?"

So, the son of a bitch smiles at Reese—doesn't even make eye contact with me—and he says, "Certainly, sir."

"I don't like that guy."

Reese says to me, "He's fine." I could hear the irritation.

"Don't tell me he's fine. He was looking at you the whole time!" Other people are staring at us now. I catch myself. "Sorry."

We're outside now, and the wind is blowing hard. What's with the weather anyway? Reese and I are waiting next to the valet stand. Remember that guy Stuart, the one who smells? Yeah, well, he's staring hard at Reese as I hand him my ticket. Instinctively, I move in as the valet gets closer.

"Reese?" he says. I can see there are tears in his eyes.

Reese ignores him, and I put myself between them. Now I'm glaring at this idiot in his black vest and ill-fitting pants. He looks ridiculous.

"You got a problem?" I say, and I grab him. "What are you staring at?"

"Go screw yourself!"

I try to live and let live, but some people have it coming. Know what I'm saying? Next thing, I'm whaling on him. Blood is gushing out his nose. He's on the ground, and I'm kicking his head like a broken parking meter.

"Stop it!" Reese says. "He wasn't doing anything! Stop it!" Meanwhile, other people are cheering me on. LA, huh?

Finally, my car arrives. Reese gets in. I'm still not played out, but Stuart isn't moving anymore, so I let him be, then throw down the ticket and twenty bucks.

"Take a shower."

"Let's go, okay?" Reese says from the car.

Is any of this resonating with you?

THINGS GET nuts back at the apartment. We're going at it pretty good. Reese is saying my name over and over.

"I can't believe how you took care of him! Oh! You—You were so good. Sooooo goooood."

No one can resist this kind of bed talk. I was an animal. After, I'm lying there wrung out. I used to smoke, so now I wish I had a cigarette.

"You are so great. It's like you know what I want."

Check it out. Reese looks at me and says, "I want it, too."

But something is still bothering me. "Listen. Did you know that guy back there at the restaurant?"

"Long time ago. Don't worry; it's nothing. I'm here for you."

I'm starting to get these deep feelings. It's too soon, but I can't help it. "I really want us to—"

"Shh," Reese says. "I want what you want. That's all. Only what you want. You're so good. Sooooo goooood."

For no reason at all, I cry—I can't help it. I'm like a baby. The tears are running hot all down Reese's body. Meanwhile, Reese is saying over and over, "Shh. It's okay. It's okay." I felt like an ass.

I don't know when I drifted off, but I had that dream again. Clouds. The squeaking noise. The fat rope inching its way over the rusty pulley. The tips of angel's wings slowly coming into view. Now I see the angel. It's me, only I'm bald and wearing an LA Angels jersey with cheap foil wings—being lifted up by the belly. I look around, and discover that the clouds are actually painted on a phony background, like some community theater production. I look up to see a huge brown rat on the rope. He's chewing through it deliberately. I hate rats.

When I wake up, I can still hear that horrible chewing

noise. Reese is gone. It's time to get ready for my presentation.

———

WE WERE MEETING in the large conference room. That made me nervous. America's Pride Adult Diapers is a new prospective account. Procter & Gamble acquired them not too long ago. The idea was, if things went well with the new brand, P&G might throw more business our way. We needed it. Things hadn't been so good for a while.

So, I'm setting up my laptop for the presentation. The table is surrounded by suits with gray hair and sour faces—you know the type. One of these faces belongs to our senior vice president. Like I said, I'm nervous as hell. My mind keeps wandering back to the previous night with Reese, only it gets all mixed up with that stupid dream. Suddenly, I hear the squeaking noise, and I'm about pass out. When I turn, I can see the catering people pushing a food cart with a bad wheel through the open doors.

The good news is, the presentation went off without a hitch. The client loved the campaign. Active seniors seizing the day and all. So, I'm heading back to my office when I see the SVP talking to my boss. I figure they're replaying my presentation. It was awesome, by the way.

Later, I'm on the phone with a director who's shooting an ad for another client. My assistant Julie comes in with a message.

"There's a Reese on the other line," she says. So, naturally, I take the call.

"Hello? Hi. No, it's fine. Tonight? Yeah, that would be great. Listen, I think I pulled it off. Just like you said. No big deal."

Later that night, I'm lying in bed with Reese.

"You should've seen that old bastard Miller," I say. "He was mesmerized."

"The client? I'll bet." Reese's voice sounds kind of funny.

"Yeah. He invited me to go sailing with him. Can you believe it?"

"So, will you get a promotion?"

"Promotion?" I hadn't even thought about that. "Yeah, I guess someday," I say. "No, right now it's brownie points. I get in good with my boss. Later, he makes it worth my while. It's like an investment."

"But you're in it for the long haul, aren't you?"

"What, are you kidding? I have to be. I'm not letting the rest of those losers get past me. No way. Hey, I put in the hours."

Then Reese gets out of bed and dresses.

"Where are you going? I thought you were going to stay over."

"I have to go. Call me tomorrow, okay?"

"Sure." This was a little strange—I'm hoping you can help me. Feel free to chime in.

Before leaving, Reese turns to me and says, "I hope you get everything you want." To be honest, I was a little creeped out.

That night, I had the dream again. Clouds. The squeaking noise. The rope inching its way over the pulley. I'm bald, and I'm being hoisted up by the belly. I look down and open my mouth to say something. Only now I have no teeth. I see someone way down below on the ground.

It's Reese.

Reese is the one controlling me. Only it's not Reese. It looks like a statue the color of bronze. And there are no eyes. Just these slit-like openings that lead into total blackness.

THE NEXT MORNING, I'm rushing to the office. The wind is blowing again. A stewbum and some woman in Armani are suddenly dancing, then are blown apart again. It's the little things, am I right?

For some reason, I have no messages. Julie informs me that my boss wants to see me. I'm thinking they want to promote me based on my presentation. So, I'm drinking coffee at my desk, reading the *Wall Street Journal*. Finally, Julie pokes her head in and tells me it's time.

My boss has the nicest office on the floor. The whole thing is decorated with antiques. I'm standing there, checking out a beautiful Chesterfield cabinet filled with photos and pricey ceramics, and I'm thinking, yeah, you killed yesterday. Here we go. My boss walks in behind me, then closes the door. Here's how it all went down. You'll like this part.

"Have a seat," he says. "Want some coffee?"

"No, thanks. Um, did Miller decide yet?"

"As a matter of fact, he did. They want to go with us."

"That's great! I had a feeling he liked me."

"Well, don't forget that Harlan did most of the work before you came on board. Solid work."

"Of course."

"But let's get on to new business. As you know, the agency hasn't done so well the last three quarters. We've been struggling pretty badly, in fact."

"Yeah, I know. That's why I've been trying to focus—"

"The thing is, to stay competitive, we've really got to cut back. You understand. I'm afraid I have to let you go."

"What?"

"Business isn't picking up the way we had hoped. It's not your fault; it's the damned economy."

"But I got you the America's Pride account!"

"I'm sorry. I wish it were different."

"I can't believe it—"

"You have a meeting with HR now to discuss your separation package. Again, I'm sorry."

It was like a nightmare. I had to suck back the tears as I cleaned out my desk. The whole time, a security guard is watching me uncomfortably.

"You don't have to breathe down my neck! I'm not going to steal anything!" I say. At least I got him to flinch.

Outside, the wind is still blowing. An inflatable sex doll shoots by and sticks to the window like it was open for business, then disappears.

Now I'm sitting behind the steering wheel of my Porsche in the parking lot, not really looking at anything. Damn thing isn't even paid off. I notice a terrified mongrel dog running in circles without reason. The thing of it is, I was on a fast track. I call Reese, but there's no answer. I go to leave a message, but I hang up instead.

FOR THE NEXT FEW HOURS, I drive around aimlessly through LA. It's getting dark. Two punks on the street hassle an old man. Some wretch, wearing a dress and a fake fox fur, pushes his shopping cart in front of my car. "Fast track," he says. Now he's giggling uncontrollably. A lonely old woman in rags pulls a couple of hollow-eyed children onto a city bus. In an alley, raccoons tear at the clothes of some stewbum who died earlier. An elderly priest makes the sign of the cross toward me as I pass his graffiti-covered church.

"Save someone who gives a shit," I say.

I end up in some rat-hole bar on Skid Row—I don't know where. There are mostly men in there. The game is on the big flat screen TV. I decide to get hammered. Over the next two hours, I take turns throwing down Johnnie Walker and calling Reese. I see that smelly valet Stuart with some of his drinking buddies. They're all dressed like valets. I turn back to the TV right when an America's Pride Adult Diaper commercial comes on. Images of happy, active geezers winning at everything appear on the screen. Here comes the tagline—my tagline: Turn "incontinent" into "confident."

The anger wells up inside me. Next thing, I'm hurling my glass at the flat screen. Well, they throw me out on my ass. I try to remember where I parked and, as I make my way past the homeless and the old winos, I'm actually cursing to myself like one of those crazy people on the street. Then Stuart appears from out of the shadows. His friends are with him. I try to focus, but I can't.

"Hey, diaper boy," he says. This strikes me as funny, and I giggle.

Now he pushes me. Okay, so now I'm scared. I try to run, but the other valets drag me into an alley.

"Lemme go!" I say. "What the hell!"

The others hold me by the arms as Stuart punches me in the face and stomach. Payback. I double over. They let me collapse to the ground. I vomit. That was it. I thought I was dead. My temple is streaming blood. I can no longer see out of my left eye. One of the other valets comes toward me with a white box—the kind you get from the laundry. He tosses it on the ground next to me. I don't know what to think. They're all standing there, waiting.

"What is it?" I say.

"Open it."

So, I pull the lid off the box. What do you think was inside? Come on. Take a guess. I'll give you a dollar. No?

A black vest.

"What?"

"It's your only way out," Stuart says.

"I don't give a loose crap what—"

"Think it over," he says. Then they leave.

The wind whistles through the alley. Groaning, I look out toward the street. A mirage-like man in a white jacket moves toward me with a silver tray. I try to focus my good eye. It's that waiter from Totentanz—Salvador! He comes over with some kind of beverage. Helps me into a sitting position.

"Come on, drink," he says. "It's iced coffee."

"I puked."

While I sit there in my own sick drinking the coffee, Salvador goes to find my car. We're in the street now where my car is waiting. He opens the passenger door and helps me inside. I look over to see who's driving.

It's Reese.

But you probably guessed that, right? Hey, don't go. This is the best part. So, Reese moves quickly through traffic now, not looking at me.

"What happened?" I say.

"You were beat up."

"What for?"

I must've drifted off. When I open my eyes, Reese has pulled over on a freeway overpass. The wind is screaming through the empty streets. It's a desert, after all. We both get out. Below, I can see cars racing in both directions. I'm delirious—rocking and looking over at all the traffic below. Reese comes up behind me. We have to scream to be heard.

"People go over all the time," I say. "People without identities. With stupid little problems nobody cares about."

"But your problems are a lot bigger, aren't they?" Reese says. "You've got so much to carry on those broad shoulders of yours."

"That's right, I do! I make a lot of money—"

"*Made* a lot of money."

"What're you contradicting me for? I thought you were on my side! I'm telling you, I'm somebody!"

"And you do things, don't you? We know how you roll, baby."

"All these responsibilities! I pay my fair share! I keep this stinking country on its feet! Not like the rest of these assholes."

"And what about all those service industries? Think of the families you're feeding. Children too poor to have milk."

"You sarcastic—"

"What's needed here is a statement. You need to lead the way for others, as you've always done in the past. Show us. Show us what it means to be a man. No, a *leader* of men."

"I should do it. Screw all of you! What does anybody care?"

"Come on. Put on the big boy pants. Show us your bravery."

Without another word, I go over. But I can still hear Reese. "It's like you said. Some people have it coming."

I saw you flinch there. It doesn't make any sense, I admit. Guy jumps the railing; next thing he's talking to me in a bar. Finish your drink. I can't wait to tell you.

I did go over, but I didn't clear the sign that's bolted to the overpass, see? I got caught on it and hung there like meat. I could hear my Porsche starting up. Always loved the sound of that car. Anyway, some driver on the freeway must've spotted me and called 911. After about ten minutes, a fire truck appears, and they pull me up just like in the dream. Then they take me to Emergency—Good Sam, I think. I find out that I have a detached retina. That's what the bandage is for. Not sure I'll ever see out of my left eye again. Whatever.

After an hour or so, I've had enough and check myself out. I have no car, and I'm on the wrong side of the 110 freeway. I can hear loud music coming out of some Mexican bar on Sixth Street. I have to get my head straight. I could've called a cab to take me back to my apartment; I still had my wallet and my credit cards. But I was feeling, I don't know, *alive*. Like I'd almost died up there on that sign. And I wanted to see how far I could take this thing. Hard to explain, but there it is.

What I needed was a gun.

It took me a long time to get here. Call it luck—whatever—I spotted my car outside this place. The keys were still in it. Pretty sloppy, I'd say.

I came in from that bitch of a wind looking for you. I thought you'd be glad to see me—happy that I wasn't dead. No? You should have checked, Reese. Made sure I'd actually fallen into traffic. I guess maybe you were tired. Understandable. I am a handful. Fortunately, as you can see, I was able to locate a gun. I'll give you a ten-minute head start for old times' sake.

Now, run.

A Bone in the Throat

IF YOU'RE GOING TO KILL YOURSELF, YOU NEED TO PUT
some thought into it. Sol considered the array of prescrip-
tion medications lined up on the kitchen counter. In the
old days, you would put your head in the oven, he remembered. Sloppy but effective. Nowadays, you used a gun. Or
pills. He didn't own a gun, and he had no intention of
going through all the mishegoss of trying to acquire one.

Sol had a lot of ailments to be sure. He was nearing
eighty-five, and since his wife Esther died, he had been in
lousy spirits. Family helped. His younger brother Ben came
over to the house regularly to cheer him up. They played
chess like they used to when they were kids, only now it
wasn't for quarters. Sometimes, Sol's nephew came along,
and they would all enjoy a game of Monopoly. He adored
his nephew.

But it was the business with the house that had finally
gotten to Sol. Bills were going unpaid. The gas company
threatened to cut him off. He didn't want to turn into a
charity case. He had always made his own money—he had
never relied on anyone. That's why he never told Ben

about his mortgage problems. Instead, he went to the bank to work things out on his own. That didn't help. Their hands were tied, they said. Nothing they could do, what with the economy. His only option was to sell.

Sol didn't want to sell. He had lived in the house—in the neighborhood—for most of his life. It was the home he bought for Esther when they married. He had waited until he had enough for a down payment, which necessitated a five-year engagement. He wasn't sure Esther would put up with it. She was a beautiful girl from Hancock Park with sparkling blue eyes and curly blonde hair. With her looks, she could have married anyone.

But she did wait for him, God bless her. She knew a good catch, he supposed. And she never complained about not having the big fancy wedding and the honeymoon on a cruise ship. It was enough for her they were married. Sweet girl.

Though they both wanted them dearly, they were never blessed with children. Sol often asked God why, and the answer was always the same. A profound silence that could have been interpreted as *It is not for you to know, Sol*, or *Why are you asking me?*

Eventually, Sol stopped asking and concentrated on working and saving enough to put his nephew through medical school since his brother couldn't afford it. Once that was accomplished, Sol thought he would retire so he and Esther could travel like they had always talked about.

Then Esther became ill.

After all the doctors and the hospitals and the operations, their nest egg had dwindled away. By the time his wife died in the hospice, Sol was left with nothing but the house and the furniture and the memories of their time together. And now even the house was in peril.

So he went to see a young man named Mr. Phillips,

who promised to get Sol out of trouble. He seemed sincere as he explained how he had done this for lots of folks like Sol. He would find a renter—giving Sol permission to remain in the house of course—and the money would take care of the mortgage payments.

It didn't work out that way.

Phillips never followed through. When Sol told the bank he could no longer make the payments, they agreed to a quick sale. After the loan was paid off, Sol could use the leftover proceeds to take a small apartment somewhere.

Then Sol learned the truth.

Those papers he had signed for Phillips to rent the house gave the stranger full ownership. He also learned Phillips had taken out a second mortgage and had already received a large check.

By the time he got his brother involved, it was too late. All the money was gone—and so was Phillips.

Sol remembered these things clearly, because his mind wasn't quite gone yet. He shuffled over to the sink and filled a glass with tap water. He brought it over to the counter and looked at the medications again. There were pills for high blood pressure, pills for his prostate, heart pills, pain pills, and cholesterol pills.

And a sedative.

Sol had a lot of trouble sleeping lately. He knew Ben was trying to help, but it was too late. And he didn't want his brother or his nephew to get involved financially. He wasn't a charity case.

He wondered what would happen if he took much more than the normal dose. He was determined to find out and pried the childproof cap off with his arthritic fingers as his heart ached over the unbelievable mistake he had made.

"I'm sorry I lost the house, Esther," he said and swallowed the first pill.

He proceeded to take one pill at a time with water until he could no longer stand. After ten or fifteen minutes, he found himself on the kitchen floor, sleepier than he had ever been in his life. This was about the time he remembered he had wanted to write a note to his brother. It was too late.

As he closed his eyes for the last time, he said, "I love you, Esther. Maybe we can play canasta when I..."

"MR. HERSHON, please feel free to make yourself comfortable." The nice-looking gentleman with the worn attaché case studied the old man to make sure he was mentally present. He had done this so many times he wanted to be certain the client was legally capable of signing the papers.

"I'm fine," the old man said. "Would you like some coffee, Mr. Kimball?"

"Sure."

"I'll make a fresh pot."

As the old man tottered toward the kitchen, Mercer took in the dining room. The house was in need of updating, although the furniture appeared to be in good shape. The wallpaper with little pastel flower baskets had a few stains on it. Hardly noticeable with all the faded family photos covering the walls. He thought he recognized some of the faces. But he had seen so many family photos over the last few years they were bound to look the same after a while.

"Do you mind if I look around?" he said.

"Help yourself."

Mercer got up and went into the living room where he found an old-fashioned walnut stereo console with a built-in TV, a La-Z-Boy recliner, and a cloth-covered sofa with white lace doilies. He remembered the old man telling him his late wife had crocheted those when they moved in.

As he wandered from room to room, appraising the bedrooms and bathrooms, he mentally added up how much cash he would soon have based on the equity. The house, as in all the other cases he had handled, was not paid off. The old man struggled to make his mortgage payments and was desperate for help. That's where Mercer came in.

He had told the old man repeatedly in those meetings at Starbucks how he was committed to helping the elderly. Why, his own mother had lost their home and ended up on the street with his younger brother and him when Mercer was only fifteen. The incident affected him deeply, and he vowed to protect others from that terrible fate.

Strolling back to the dining room, Mercer was convinced he had made the right choice in taking on this client. He was certain he would have signed papers tonight, and tomorrow, he could start the loan process, giving himself a couple hundred thousand in cash, easy. He sat at the table as the old man brought out a silver tray with a silver coffeepot and china cups.

"Were those wedding gifts?" Mercer said.

"Yes. I still like to use them. They remind me of my late wife."

"Very nice." Mercer waited patiently as the old man poured the coffee with trembling hands.

Sipping his coffee, the old man looked at Mercer with rheumy eyes. "I'm so pleased you decided to help me rent my place," he said.

"Yes, so am I," Mercer said as he arranged all of the paperwork on the table. "Dammit!"

"What's wrong?"

"Can you believe it? I forgot a pen." Mercer was genuinely embarrassed; it wasn't like him.

"It happens," the old man said, waving his hand.

He got up and went into the kitchen. Could he move any slower? Mercer seethed. Finally, Hershon returned with a blue ballpoint pen with the name of an insurance company printed on the barrel. He also carried a bottle of Fundador.

"Thanks," Mercer said.

"I thought you'd like some brandy for the coffee. In Spain, they call it *con gotas*."

"No thanks," Mercer said.

"Well, I'm having some," the old man said and poured about two fingers into his cup.

"You know, why not?" Mercer said and slid his cup over. "This is a happy occasion, after all."

"It sure is," Hershon said as he poured. "And you say you'll take care of everything?"

"That's right. Your signing these papers authorizes me to rent the house for you. I've already included a provision stating that you can remain here as long as you live. I plan to use one of the bedrooms for myself and maybe the study, if you don't mind."

"No, no, sounds fine. I don't need much," the old man said, smiling. "And it will be good to have some company. Do you play chess?"

"Not really."

"Is it chilly in here?" Hershon said.

"I'm very comfortable."

"I'm sorry, Mr. Kimball, but this weather aggravates my arthritis. I hope you don't mind if I light the fire."

"Be my guest."

Mercer watched with irritation as the old man got up again, shuffled over to the fireplace, and turned on the gas. A bright blue-orange flame licked its way up through the cement logs. Hershon warmed his hands there momentarily, came back, and sat down.

"That's better," he said. "Sorry for the interruption."

"Now, here are the papers you need to sign," Mercer said. "I've already put little yellow arrows where your signature goes. And you'll be getting a complete set of the documents for your records."

"Good," the old man said.

Mercer wasn't sure, but the old man actually seemed to be looking forward to this. "Now, Mr. Hershon," he said, "let's get started."

Mercer got butterflies. It always happened when he was about to reap a windfall. He had been doing this for five years now, and he was the best. How many clients had he scammed? Was it twenty-four or twenty-seven? He couldn't remember exactly.

He had begun his new career in Florida when his name was Finch. Things were really bad there, and he did well. But when the complaints came in and the authorities began investigating, he hightailed it and came west to Kansas City. Eventually, he moved on, hitting Denver, Billings, Phoenix, and now Los Angeles. He skipped Las Vegas, because, frankly, he was afraid of crossing paths with organized crime. Even someone as good as he was had to be careful.

Los Angeles was perfect. Everything was so spread out. He could easily go from one depressed community to another, pulling the same scam. All he had to do was change his name every six months and move on. He was now known as Frank Kimball.

He had already amassed quite a lot of money, which he had deposited in several offshore accounts. But he wasn't flashy. That was a mistake amateurs made. He did nothing to attract attention. Even his name was forgettable. He currently drove a used Honda Civic and wore off-the-rack suits from JCPenney. His shoes had rubber soles, and he wore no jewelry except for a Timex watch with a brown leatherette band. He lived in a nondescript one-bedroom apartment in Torrance and paid cash for everything. He was, in his own opinion, the picture of ordinariness. This helped him present a trustworthy appearance.

Whenever he met a new prospect, he often talked about his late wife, who had been tragically killed by a drunk driver. They had only been married a year. Although he would like to remarry, he was too involved in church work at the present time. Maybe the right girl would turn up someday. People, he noticed, loved that crap. And he served it up in a slop pail.

"What was your wife's name again?" the old man said.

"Lillian," Mercer said. "She went by Lilly."

"Such a pretty name. Something wrong?"

Mercer felt strange. The sensation was unlike anything he had ever felt. He hoped he wasn't getting sick.

"Just a little lightheaded," he said. "Must be the brandy."

"Have some more coffee," the old man said. "This time I'll leave the brandy out."

"Okay," Mercer said and drained his cup.

He watched as Hershon tried reading the fine print on each of the documents. "That's just an indemnity clause," Mercer said. "Pretty standard."

"Maybe I should call my son to help me," the old man said.

Not a good sign, Mercer thought. He might have to

abort. You never wanted an outside party involved, especially one he hadn't already vetted. Anything might happen. The son might have an attorney and insist on having the papers reviewed. Or worse, he might *be* an attorney.

He recalled the time he had conned an old couple in Phoenix. Right before he was to drive over to the couple's condo so they could sign the papers, the husband called and said Mercer should meet them at his son's law office. He remembered the threatening tone of the man's voice— like he already knew. Mercer never showed up. Instead, he used the opportunity to get the hell out of Dodge.

Mercer tried getting to his feet to leave, but found he couldn't stand. What was happening? Was it some kind of virus? His head felt funny, and there was a tingling in his arms and legs.

"I have another appointment," he said. He was slurring his speech and drooling. Was he having a stroke? "So if you want your son to look over the paperwork, I'm afraid we'll have to reschedule," he said.

"No, we can take care of it now," the old man said. "My son lives next door in the little bungalow you saw when you drove up."

"Uh-huh," Mercer said, his body becoming weaker.

"I'll just call him. Only take a minute."

Mercer watched as the old man struggled to his feet and went into the kitchen to make the call. He could hear part of the conversation. It was hard, because, apparently, the dishwasher was running. He gathered the son's name was Barry or Larry.

When the old man returned, Mercer could no longer move or speak. He was completely, utterly still. The only things functioning were his eyelids, which fluttered frantically.

"Gary will be right over," Hershon said. "Ah, I think I hear him now."

Mercer listened as the back door opened with a squeak and a voice said, "Pop?"

"In here, son!"

Mercer could tell the old man loved his son dearly. He tried to remember if his own father had ever acted in a similar way toward him. There was one time when he was three and his father held his hand as they went outside to buy ice cream from the truck.

Another man, around thirty, stepped into the dining room. He was wearing a sport coat, slacks, and a tie, and carried a doctor's bag. He appeared frighteningly professional.

"Mr. Kimball, this is my son Gary. Gary, Mr. Kimball. He's the one who's going to help me with the house."

"Pleased to meet you," Gary said and extended his hand.

Mercer failed to move a muscle. Instead, he made a gurgling noise and stared at Gary stupidly.

"Kind of rude, isn't he?" Gary said to his father as he took a seat at the table. "Now, let's see what we have here."

The son went through the papers, moving his lips as he read the fine print. All Mercer could do was watch and wait.

"More coffee, Mr. Mercer?" the old man said.

Gary set the papers down, folded his hands, and leaned forward. His expression changed from one of a genial smiling rube to that of a hanging judge about to hand down a sentence.

"I'm no lawyer," Gary said, "but I have to say, based on what I see in these documents, you are trying to take advantage of my father."

Mercer's eyes became huge. He would have given

anything to be able to get up and run. All he could do was emit a pathetic squeak.

"Sorry, I didn't hear you," Gary said. "I just can't imagine another scenario where you come out looking good in this thing, Kimball. If my father signs these papers, you gain full control of the title. It says so right here. And although you verbally promised him you would rent the house, there is nothing in here to indicate that. So, theoretically, you could renege, apply for a line of credit, and take out every drop of equity my poor father has, leaving him penniless of course." He turned to his father. "Sorry if this is a shock to you, Pop."

Mercer closed his eyes, trying to block out the reality of what was happening, but he couldn't shut off his hearing.

"No, I'm afraid it won't do, Kimball," Gary said. "I'm canceling the deal."

He gathered up the papers, took them over to the fireplace, opened the glass doors, and tossed them in. Mercer watched as his con went up in flames. Three weeks' work gone. He had turned away two other prospects—good prospects—because he was so sure this one would pay off big. And now, he had nothing except ashes to show for his effort.

Gary returned to the table, stroked his father's head, and gave him a kiss.

"Family is everything to me," he said. "After my mother passed, I focused all my attention on keeping my father safe. I look after his health, make sure he eats right, and see to it that nothing bad happens to him."

Mercer opened his eyes and realized Gary had opened his doctor's bag and was now laying out surgical equipment on the table. Tears blinded Mercer momentarily, but he was certain one of the instruments was a dangerous-looking surgical saw. It was slightly larger than an electric toothbrush, made of stainless steel, with a round blade with little holes all the way around.

"I'll tell you what really hurts though," Gary said. "My parents were too poor to pay for medical school. But my uncle Sol—Dad's older brother—wasn't. He wanted to make sure I had the life he felt I deserved. And he had the pleasure of seeing me complete my studies and become a top-rated surgeon here in the Los Angeles area."

"Did you remember the drop cloths?" the old man said.

"Right!"

Gary ran into the kitchen and came back with a huge roll of thick clear plastic he used to cover the dining-room table. He expertly used an X-ACTO knife to slice it. Next, he dragged Mercer's chair back—with Mercer still in it—and covered the floor with plastic. After everything was well protected, he moved Mercer back into position.

Mercer tried with all his strength to scream. He could hear his own voice inside his head, but no one else could.

"You're probably wondering why you can't move," Gary said as he completed the inspection of his instruments, removed his jacket, and slipped on blue surgical scrubs. "Originally, I had planned to use suxamethonium chloride. Of course, the problem with that drug is its effects wear off in minutes. And I need you immobile for much longer."

Gary went over to Mercer and felt around in his jacket pockets. He grabbed the car keys and smiled. "Dad, I'm just going to move his car into the garage. Be back in a sec."

Mercer couldn't believe it. His eyes pleaded with the old man, but Hershon just sat there, smiling like an idiot. He got up—much sprightlier now, Mercer noticed—and cleared away the coffee things. Had Mercer been played?

Gary returned minutes later and peered into Mercer's pupils with a small flashlight. Next, he checked Mercer's pulse and finished up the exam by listening to his heart with a stethoscope.

"The problem with other kinds of anesthesia is you become unconscious. Also, you tend not to feel any pain. This is not at all what we want. Fortunately, science comes to the rescue. A few months ago, my pharmaceutical rep told me about a new experimental drug. It completely paralyzes the patient—except for the breathing, of course —but keeps the patient conscious and fully aware of everything. It took some doing, but I was able to secure a sufficient quantity. This is what my father gave you." He chuckled. "I bet you thought it was in the brandy. It wasn't. It was in the coffee. My dad used the brandy to cover up the taste."

Mercer could feel his heart racing with adrenaline, but could do nothing about it. He heard himself scream again, which came out as an almost imperceptible whimper.

"Don't try to speak," Gary said. "You'll exhaust yourself. And I want you relaxed and rested when I operate."

Gary plugged an extension cord into the wall and connected it to the surgical saw. He tested it in the light, the motor whirring efficiently like a dentist's drill.

"My father and I did some research. Actually, I lied. We hired a private investigator who built up quite a file on you. Your real name is John Mercer. Both your parents are deceased, and you were never married nor do you have a sibling. You're twenty-seven years old, and you have never, to anyone's knowledge, made an honest living.

"Unfortunately, Mercer, I am unable to exact retribution for all your victims, but I can at least account for…twenty-one? Yes, twenty-one. It is some measure of justice. Especially where Uncle Sol is concerned."

He knelt down and removed Mercer's shoes and socks. Then he went into the kitchen to wash up, came back, and applied Betadine liberally to Mercer's hands and feet. Mercer could feel the cold sensation of the reddish-brown liquid.

"I'll apologize in advance—I don't have a nurse," Gary said. "So I might be a little slow stanching the bleeding. But I'll do my best not to let you bleed out. I'll begin with your fingers—one for each of your victims. Then, once I've bandaged those properly, I'll continue with your toes.

"Normally I'm not in favor of strangers putting their feet on the table, but in this case, I can make an exception. Fingers and toes. That's twenty. You're probably wondering what number twenty-one is. That's a surprise."

Mercer tried to will his heart to stop. He wanted desperately to die, but it stubbornly kept beating stronger than ever.

"Dad, can you bring over a garbage bag?" Gary said.

"Sure, Gary. What will you do with all the dead flesh?"

"Oh, I think I won't have any trouble getting to the incinerator at the hospital."

"He's a smart boy, my son," Hershon said as Gary put on a surgical mask.

"Now, Mr. Mercer," Gary said, "let's get started."

MERCER'S ROOM was quite pleasant. It overlooked the Pacific Ocean. The sun was just going down. The windows were open, and the white curtains billowed gently from a warm breeze. It felt good.

He hoped the orderly would bring his food soon, because he was getting hungry. These last few weeks had given him time to reflect on everything that had happened. Now sitting in the wicker chair by the window, he raised his arms and looked at what used to be his almost-perfect hands. Piano hands, his mother had once called them, although they could never afford lessons. Now they resembled flesh-colored paddles with little nubs sticking out. The skin was smooth and shiny with scar tissue where the Mexican surgeon had expertly repaired what was left of his fingers.

The pain was almost gone. And so were the nightmares. Until recently, he had relived those horrible few hours nightly. The drug—whatever it was—had allowed him to do nothing more than breathe and blink his eyes. But it had done something else. It has sharpened his senses to the point where every sound was magnified, every sensation achingly bright.

The first finger was the worst. He heard the saw and felt it slicing cleanly through at the joint connecting to the hand. He remembered Gary saying something about a carbon blade as he tossed the finger into the garbage bag. Again, in his mind, he screamed in agony. And so it was with each of his ten fingers. He had wanted to pass out as Gary went to work on his toes.

Mercer remembered a lot of blood, too. It was the blood and the screaming and the smell of the burning bone that tore through his dark dreams and left him weak and exhausted in the morning. But the dreams were fading now like the scars on his hands.

He examined his bare feet once again. They too seemed like elongated paddles. And like his hands, everything was smooth and shiny where his toes used to be.

He was tired of sitting and almost decided to get up from the chair. But after past repeated attempts, he knew he would just end up falling forward, maybe even going out the window. There was no way for him to balance without toes. He was in effect a cripple.

However, the thing Mercer thought about most—especially during the quiet evenings overlooking the sea—was how he ended up in the situation. This was the mental exercise that plagued him daily. He struggled to pinpoint the exact time in his life when he went from a quiet loner to a desperate con man.

Was it his father's death when he was fifteen? It would be easy to blame everything on that. But wasn't he already conning kids out of their lunch money in middle school? Never the bully, he would devise elaborate cons involving playground games, girls' lockers, and PE showers. Over time, the other kids looked forward to his schemes and gladly handed over their money as the admission price for the show.

In fifth grade, he won a speech contest sponsored by the local Rotary Club. He was eleven and had found out quite by accident that his father was cheating on his mother. He always had a facility for persuasion. If he hadn't become a con, he might have gone into politics.

Was it fourth grade? No, because at that time, he lied about everything. Never for money though. Just the normal reasons like not doing his homework and getting out of chores at home.

In second grade, he kissed Melody Levinsohn. She liked it, too, and pursued him the rest of the year. In third grade, she forgot who he was and focused on her schoolwork. Is that when it happened? No, because he was already stealing candy from the corner liquor store.

Had he been born bad?

He thought about kindergarten. It was called the Little Red Schoolhouse. He was five and had never to his recollection been in school before. This was where his memory grew fuzzy. He tried to recall the faces of the other children and the teacher, but it was hopeless. He remembered playing with Tinker Toys and Legos. He recalled a ventriloquist's dummy that sat on a bookshelf. Sometimes, the teacher would use the dummy for storytelling.

Then he saw it in his mind as clear as day.

He had been playing on the carpet with a Tonka truck. Another boy wanted the truck and tried taking it away. Mercer refused to give it up. Where had the teacher been? The boy kept pulling at the truck. Because he was bigger, he was able to get it away from Mercer and hit him over the head with it.

Mercer screamed as blood poured from a nasty cut on his head. He could still remember the look of complete disinterest on the other boy's face as the teacher took him away to the office and another adult—the nurse?—attended to Mercer.

He hadn't done anything wrong. He was just playing. He had not been bad.

There was a knock. The orderly came in and he brought the food. Mercer's stomach growled as he smelled the savory rice with chicken broth and bits of meat and vegetables. The orderly put a bib on him and fed him with a spoon. The chicken and vegetables had to be cut up very small so Mercer wouldn't choke.' It was still hard to chew, so he mostly swallowed.

The last time Mercer saw Gary was here at the clinic. Mercer was in bad shape—almost unconscious and in shock, his hands and feet wrapped in bloody bandages. Gary had spoken Spanish with the admitting nurse and signed a pile of papers. Mercer wasn't certain, but he had the impression these Mexicans thought he was Gary's ward.

Even without fingers, Mercer was able to grasp the

plastic cup filled with ice-cold limeade and bring the straw to his lips without spilling a drop. He liked limeade. He knew he would probably never see Gary again. What he didn't know was how long he would remain in this purgatory.

He remembered Gary's words to him just before he left. Mercer would be here for a time, but one day, the orderly would enter the room and, instead of bringing food, would throw him out the window to a silent death on the rocks below. He would never know when. It could be tomorrow; it could be in ten years. Mercer wouldn't know until it happened. And that ate at him.

"It's like a bone in your throat," Gary had said. "It doesn't kill you, but you can't stop thinking about it."

Mercer would have liked to ask someone in charge how long. He would have liked to know his fate. He would have liked to have the facts so he could decide whether life was worth living. But he couldn't ask anyone. And it wasn't because he could not write or because he didn't know any Spanish.

He couldn't ask, because the last thing—the twenty-first thing—Gary took was his tongue.

Regino Sings

REGINO HAD BEEN SUFFERING FOR A LONG TIME WITH THE cancer. Now, it was at the point where he could no longer function as a regular human being. He drooled constantly. Eating was a problem.

The doctor told him it was time for the operation they had discussed so many months ago. It frightened Regino to think he would have a mechanical mouth and not the lovely soft pink cradle he was born with. But unless he went through with it, he would die.

His mother, Isabel, drove him to the hospital early in the afternoon. Though she couldn't see very well, she refused to wear glasses. Regino was afraid she would hit a kid or a dog.

"Don't let them take your clothes away," she said. "What'll you do if there's a fire?"

He couldn't answer because the large fleshy gray lump that had sprung from the roof of his mouth prevented him. So, he sucked on it in silence.

At the hospital, the nurse took all of Regino's vital information from Isabel who was only too happy to provide details. He had never been the sort of person to blush. But he turned crimson as his mother confided to the nurse that her son had never married and consequently was a little virgin, and could that have anything to do with the cancer in his mouth? The nurse didn't know but promised to mention it to the doctor.

Isabel kissed Regino on the small indentation in his forehead as she had done for fifty years and said goodbye. Just as soon as he got into his semi-private room, they took away all of his clothes and left him with a diaphanous hospital gown. He thanked God no one was in the other bed.

The operation would begin at seven in the morning. At six, Regino would be given an injection to induce sleep and "dry him up." By ten, it would all be over, and he would be ready for his new mouth.

The development of the prosthetic device was remarkable in that it had been invented by an ex-ventriloquist named Vrolo who claimed to have thought of it after seeing bright lights in the sky. After years of studying speech pathology, engineering, and computer science, Vrolo successively built more complicated prototypes.

For his trouble, he was awarded a patent and eventually sold his machine to a global medical devices company for ten million dollars. Unfortunately, Vrolo went mad, and the proceeds had to be spent on constant care inside the walls of a great, gibbering booby hatch somewhere in the Midwest.

Regino recalled the glossy sales brochures. The device ran on a state-of-the-art nuclear battery and contained a powerful microprocessor. Another chip contained all the known words of the English language according to the Oxford English Dictionary and could be updated with wireless downloads from the Internet. Other chips could be added later for foreign languages.

He thought about all of the lovely new words he would be able to use and how nice it would be to speak like a poet. He recalled famous speeches he could recite and dark, brooding technical articles he might like to quote. He thought of love.

The doctor warned Regino there would be a lot of postoperative pain at first and how he would be unable to speak to anyone. That was fine with Regino because he knew the first person he would lay eyes on when he awoke was his meddling mother.

They had given him a mild sedative. He dozed off around ten. When he awoke the next morning, he found a nurse preparing to inject him.

"Do you have to tinkle, Mr. Lopez?" she said.

"Yeszth."

Then, without warning, she gave it to him in the ass.

"Just rest there, and someone will come for you in around forty-five minutes."

He had hoped Dr. Shapiro would stop by to give him all kinds of reassurances. But the only people he saw were orderlies delivering breakfast to other patients and nurses prattling on about their sleazy ex-husbands and unmanageable teenage sons.

Some time later—he didn't know when—two orderlies arrived and wheeled a gurney next to his bed. Then, they slid Regino sideways onto the gurney, sheets and all, and quickly wheeled him down the corridor. His head was spinning.

"How do you feel?" someone said.

"Woozshy."

"It'll be over soon."

He waited in another corridor for twenty more

minutes. Finally, someone pushed him into the operating room, which was very cold. They covered him in a blanket, and he was grateful.

The anesthesiologist was fiddling with incomprehensible instruments and dials. He said very little except to tell Regino he was about to run an IV. Thickly, Regino watched as a needle was inserted into his forearm and taped there. His eyes followed the clear plastic hose and saw that it fed into a plastic sack filled with liquid. He spotted a valve. The anesthesiologist turned it, and Regino's life ended for a while.

REGINO AWOKE IN ANOTHER ROOM. It seemed no time at all had passed, and the operation would soon begin. Then he fell asleep again.

When he opened his eyes, he was back in his room. Isabel was there, knitting fiercely and scowling at the sick and injured who passed by as if they had no right to exist.

"They took your clothes," she said without dropping a stitch. "What did I tell you, Regino? How do you feel?"

It hurt. It hurt like nothing he'd ever felt in his life, including that time the old redwood garage door fell on his head and split it open. It hurt bad.

"Nain!" he said.

"Pain? Yes, I thought so. Look."

She removed a pink plastic hand mirror from the huge canvas knitting bag and shoved it in his face. What he saw was a crater swaddled in blood-soaked bandages. His chin and lower jaw were missing. All that remained was flapping skin.

"Augh!"

On cue, a nurse appeared and snatched the mirror

away. "You shouldn't upset him like that," she said. "He needs his rest if he's going to recover."

"My mou?"

"It's all right, Ruhgeeno," she said, her voice childlike all of a sudden. "They're programming it now. Tomorrow morning, if God's will, it will be fitted to your skull. Today, they had to remove all of those bad old parts and implant the steel pins. Soon, they'll hook up your new mouth. Now, then. Who wants a nice, cold orange soda?"

The nurse glared at Isabel and left the room, still carrying the mirror.

"I want that back when I leave!" Isabel said, humiliated for perhaps the first time in her life. And it's pronounced *ReHEENo!* Bitch."

Regino wept. He sobbed to think that the teeth he grew up with, the chin he had so lovingly shaved for so long, were gone forever. Burned in the hospital incinerator by now probably. And what about all those gold fillings?

"I made them give me all the fillings," his mother said.

She opened her palm and dumped them onto the little tray next to the water pitcher. They were dirty-colored and misshapen.

He cried some more.

AS THE WEEKS PASSED, the pain lessened. Dr. Shapiro was very pleased that Regino's body had not rejected the false mouth. Soon, he was eating solid food again and smiling in the bathroom mirror through new, perfectly straight white teeth.

Strangely, as he learned to speak through the machine, his voice deepened. It took on a rich, resonant quality it had never had in his younger years. His mother hated it because, in contrast, it made hers sound nasal and irritating.

Life was fun again. Regino read books. He watched old movies. Soon, new healthy skin completely covered the mechanical parts, and his mouth appeared natural. Except he was always aware of the whirring of tiny motors in his ears conducted through the bone and amplified. Occasionally, he picked up radio broadcasts.

"'It was the best of times, it was the worst of times, it was the age of wisdom, it was the age of foolishness.' *A Tale of Two Cities.*"

"I know what it is, Regino," Isabel said. "You sound like a radio announcer."

"'I haven't lived a good life. I've been bad. Worse than you could know.'"

"Stop it, you're making me angry."

"'I won't be innocent.' *The Maltese Falcon.*"

One day while Regino was reciting Shelley, he skipped a few articles, then a pronoun. At first, he thought it was his eyes and used his reading glasses. Rereading the passage, the problem appeared to go away.

"What do you want for lunch?" Isabel said through the bathroom door as her son bathed.

"I'd like a bowl soup."

"You've done it again. You've forgotten the 'of.'"

She was right—it was happening again. A missing word here and there. Something was wrong with his new mouth. He had *thought* the "of."

"I'd like a bowl soup."

No, the "of" was definitely gone. Regino tried other phrases.

"Sackful dreams. Cup coffee. United States America." The "of," it seemed, had permanently left his mouth's memory.

It was Friday night. Dr. Shapiro would be out of town for the weekend. Regino would have to manage somehow. After slurping frantically at his soup, he hit upon the idea of substituting "off" for "of."

"I'd like another bowl off soup," he said. He felt sure that if he said it fast enough, no one would notice.

"That sentence doesn't make sense," Isabel said, laughing.

He became enraged at her braying insensitivity. "I'd like another bowl off soup!"

"I'll give you more soup when you ask for it properly. What do you think *off* that?"

He hit her. It was the first time. And the stinging look of shock and rage that welled in Isabel's eyes filled him, too, with shame and a kind of spent hubris.

"Mother!"

She left the house. Choosing to ignore her tantrum, he inserted a probe into his ear to check for radiation leakage.

DAYS WENT BY. At first, Regino worried his mother had gotten into some kind of trouble. Then, he remembered the time she left his father for a week. Eventually, she called them from Puerto Vallarta. Regino's father had wept openly on the telephone and promised to try and be a better husband.

Regino didn't cry, though. Instead, he ate meatball sandwiches from the Butcher Boy deli and drank beer out of bottles. Isabel hated beer—the smell of it. And she hated what it did to men sometimes. Once, Regino's father had gotten very drunk and urinated on the carpet to the utter horror of his Wagnerian wife. Later, he claimed it was an accident. Not the urinating. That was deliberate.

Regino's father had gotten drunk by accident because a coworker had died. The office decided to go and have a drink in his honor. Then, they honored him three more times. Three more bars and six hours later, they had bestowed upon their dead comrade *la Légion d'honneur*. Regino's father was not a good drinker.

COUSIN FELIX SHOWED up on Tuesday looking for Isabel. Regino hated him because he was handsome and didn't have a false mouth. He also hated Felix because he was successful. Felix owned a string of gas stations and never once got his hands greasy. He left that to his aged father who wore three trusses and a black patch to cover his lazy eye, which, Felix insisted, frightened the customers.

"What have you done with her?" Felix said, helping himself to garlic olives, pretzels, and beer.

"She's just gone away flor a few days."

"Mouth acting up again?" Felix's teeth were capped, Regino was sure of it. "You ought to bring your kisser over to my station. I'll have Dad take a look at it. You know, put it on the scope. Prob'ly just needs a little grease."

That was it. Regino opened his mouth as wide as it would go and let out one clear, crisp note so high and sweet and ethereal, it gave Felix a nosebleed.

"Cut it out!" Felix said, trying to stanch the bubbling brain-blood gushing down his lavender silk shirt.

But Regino liked his sudden talent and continued to sing. Felix became woozy and fell to his knees. Blood began seeping from his ears. It was as if his head were in a microwave oven. He was sure he would be dead soon.

"Bastard," he said and lost consciousness.

When he awoke, Felix was lying on a small cot inside

Isabel's pantry. Cans of tomato sauce and lima beans scowled at him. His head throbbed miserably. He could barely see. His nose and ears had been stopped up with wadded-up bulk cotton.

"Regino?" he said.

Regino looked in through the little window in the door, his eyes smiling viciously.

Later when Felix was able to walk, Regino helped him to his Escalade and, through the use of sparse erudite body language, told him to go straight to hell.

"I'm going to report you, you bastard!" Felix said as he threw the car into reverse.

"I'll sing."

Regino opened his mouth, about to reach for the note that could make the saints weep. Felix screamed and blasted backward out of the driveway, taking a neighbor kid's tricycle with him.

"*Pendejo,*" Regino said and went back inside to order a meatball sandwich.

REGINO CALLED the manufacturer of his mouth and explained to the customer service representative in Manila about the singing. The agent claimed he never heard of it and referred Regino to some electronics company in Singapore. After repeated calling across several continents, Regino gave up.

Apparently, the singing was an undocumented feature of the mouth. It was not referenced in any of the manuals he'd received, and it wasn't a malfunction. It was cruel magic.

Regino remembered reading somewhere that the inventor had gone mad, and he decided to pay the man a visit. Helping himself to Isabel's credit cards, he booked a flight to Fort Wayne, Indiana, where he knew Mr. Vrolo was recuperating.

Though Vrolo was only fifty—the same as Regino—he looked ninety. His hair was close-cropped and white. His eyes were a kind of blue metallic china. Intense, seeing everything and nothing. Set beneath a thunderhead of wiry eyebrows and brooding beetle-browed unfor-giveness.

"You're wearing my mouth," Vrolo said. "Tell me, have you sung lately?"

The inventor was apparently having a private joke at Regino's expense. His eyes gamboled like cold, blue flames.

"I have sung a strange and wonderful song," Regino said. "But I don't know why. And it *hurts* people."

"Yes, it does." Vrolo's look became discerning as if he were sizing up Regino for the job of Savior of the World (for which there just happened to be an opening). "And?"

"And I almost killed my cousin Felix."

"Good. But you really ought to learn to control it," Vrolo said. "To refine it. It comes to you raw, you see, filled with promise and dread. But it can be taught to be useful. You'll see."

"I don't know what you mean. What are you talking about?"

"It's the Angels' Song. I discovered it by accident."

"You mean, the mouth?"

"Yes. It's programmed in. Part of the works. Can't function otherwise. Company knows nothing about it, the fools. It'll kill."

Regino looked on in a kind of gentle horror born of dark desire as Vrolo opened his mouth and let out a soft, elucidous whisper of a note, so light and killing it made a doddering, palsy-ridden old man in the corner of the room dance like Fred Astaire momentarily, then collapse into a viscous liquid coma.

"There now. Get the hell away from me and let my madness alone. Wait! Have you seen any bright lights?"

Regino stumbled out of the day room as orderlies rushed in to help the old man who was by now quite dead. His mind crammed with possibilities, he flew home to practice.

FELIX DIDN'T LIKE what he saw. There was Isabel on a ladder, painting the front of the house. She seemed to be smiling. He adjusted the huge headphones padded with drugstore gauze and got out of the car.

"Everything looks perfectly normal to me," said his friend and fellow Rotarian, Police Captain Putzmeister.

"What?"

"I said everything— Oh, never mind."

They wandered up the walkway, Putzmeister admiring the house and Felix glowering with a loathing suspicion.

"Hello, Aunt Isabel!"

She nodded and smiled some more, then continued painting a world of her own. Regino answered the door wearing a new cashmere sweater, wool slacks, and four hundred dollar shoes. He was heavier and had a rosy goose liver pâté disposition.

"Uh, Regino, this is Capt. Putzmeister. He's here to drag your guilty ass off to jail."

"Hold on now, Felix," Putzmeister said, chuckling amiably. "Nobody's dragging anybody anywhere. This is America. May we come in?"

Graciously, Regino admitted them and stopped to check on Isabel. "Don't forget under the eaves, *mami*."

"I won't, sweetheart!"

The house was different. Felix gawped at the new furniture, expensive electronic equipment, and serigraphs on the wall depicting lusty European women in compromising positions dominated by swarthy, slick-looking men wearing tuxedos and holding bullwhips.

"What've you done to her?" he said. Regino gazed sympathetically at Putzmeister.

"Uh, Felix seems to have the idea you've, uh, 'done' something to your mother. Heh-heh. You know, threatened her or something."

"What?" Felix said.

"Look, will you take those damned things off!" Putzmeister yanked the headphones off Felix's head.

"Ow!"

"Now, I don't know about you, Felix. But I see nothing wrong here. Everything looks just fine to me."

"No, no, no! I told you in the car. It's that voice. He's *done* something to her. With the *voice!* Look at all this stuff!"

"Hm. Uh, Mr. Lopez, do you sing?"

Regino smiled self-consciously. "Why, yes, Captain. I was just getting ready to practice when you came in. Do you like Schubert?"

"Are you kidding? I *love* Schubert!"

Confidently, Regino went to the new grand piano and slid out a drawer from underneath the keyboard. Then, he put in a disc. The piano began to play "Ständchen." And Regino, his mouth no longer plagued by software glitches, serenaded the two men—but mostly the cop—in German.

He performed the deep abiding sadness that Putzmeister had never heard before. He intoned the closeness of it, the heart's gentle yearning. He sang the hell out of it.

When it was over, Putzmeister blew his nose and wiped

his eyes. "That was beautiful! As fine as anything Fischer-Dieskau ever recorded."

Felix didn't hear because as soon as Regino had opened his mouth, he jostled the headphones back on. "Let's get out of here," he said.

"Thank you, Mr. Lopez. Sorry to have bothered you."

"No bother, Captain. Come over for dinner sometime, and I'll sing some more for you. I'm working on Verdi."

"What a talent!"

Outside, Isabel had fallen off the ladder and broken her arm. A jagged piece of bone bathed in a pink film was sticking out of the skin in an altogether unwholesome manner.

Felix ran to her. "Aunt Isabel!"

"Oh, my," she said and fainted.

AFTER RETURNING FROM THE ER, Regino decided to give his mother the rest of the day off. Then, noshing on cold salmon and imported beer, he thought of ways to perform his microsurgery on more people.

Vrolo was right. You had to learn to control the voice. In its feral form, it could ruin a person—drive him out of his mind. But purified, it could perform delicate alterations of the brain's structure, accomplishing what lobotomists had only dreamed of.

Like a delicate laser, you could focus the instrument on specific areas of the brain. You could dissect here, cauterize there. You could make a violent person calm, a milquetoast bold, a domineering land shark with a taste for blood sweet.

Regino didn't want his mother destroyed. Far from it. After all, she had all the money, and he needed her to continue writing checks. So he read anatomy books and practiced on neighborhood dogs and cats. At first, the wretches died of madness. Then, he learned to think sweet thoughts. That helped some, and they only bled to death from brain hemorrhages.

After months of work, he was ready to try it out on Isabel. She had returned only a week before, tanned and rested. She had lost weight and intended to file charges against her son for assault and battery. Somehow, though, she never got around to it. Once surrounded by the familiar objects of her ivory life, she settled down.

But she was still abusive. She needled Regino and laughed cruelly at his attempts to better himself. She wondered how much Felix made last year after taxes and how many girls his strapping teenage boys were having sex with. She thought she and Felix's family ought to go on a cruise together.

It was during *The Bold and the Beautiful* that Regino made his move. Surprisingly, it didn't take long. Just a few seconds here at the commercial break, a few seconds there. By the time the program was over, Isabel was different. And the best part: she didn't appear to notice the change.

Regino had only to sigh in her direction, and she would fix him a meal fit for King Edward. He kissed her, and she pulled out her checkbook to write any amount he wanted. She tucked him in at night and ironed his underwear in the morning. He had it made.

Now, there would be girls at the house and music and parties. He had only to use the voice. And politics! Why not? He could run for mayor and live in a big country house. Then governor, then President of the United States!

These were only some of the things Regino dreamed of in his room at night as he savaged himself. He thought of monumental decisions vis-à-vis the fate of the world.

Trips to the great capitals. Thunderous applause. Too bad Vrolo went loopy. Poor bastard. He just didn't have the stomach for it.

But why waste time with small-town politics? Why not get it over with and do everyone? Oh, this was great. He had to think. Why not go on the radio—no, *television*—and sing in the horrible, sweet voice that would bend men, women, and children to his will? They would worship him and give him things just as the defeated, simpering Isabel lived to do.

Oh, this was devilish. Regino wished he could tell Vrolo so they could laugh together over it. Why not call him?

"Mr. Lopez, I'm sorry to inform you that Mr. Vrolo has passed away."

"What!" he said, collapsing on the bed.

"It was very sudden. We're all still a bit shaken."

"B-but how..."

"Well, seeing you're a friend, I'm afraid he killed himself. In the hospital bakery. You see, we had been letting him work there the past few weeks. It seemed to relax him.

"And one morning we found him in the ginormous mixer twisted in and around the beaters. He-he'd been making musical bread!" She was crying all over again. "It took the firemen hours to get him out. Of course, the service was closed casket."

"Stupid fool!" Regino said and hung up.

He hated Vrolo. The thought of him sickened Regino. He wanted to rip someone's heart out. Fortunately, Isabel was out buying him a black forest cake.

Now, all of his energy—every waking moment—would have to be spent planning his coup. How could he get on television? A commercial! He could buy time just like the beer and diaper companies did. But his commercial would have to be broadcast nationally. And it would have to run on all of the major networks at the same time. That would take lots of money.

He went into his room to work out his plan. He didn't even come out to eat. The next day, he called all the networks to find out their advertising rates during prime time. Hundreds of thousands of dollars! Well, you have to spend money to make money. After this, he would reap *millions*.

Regino hadn't even considered the cost of making the commercial. He knew nothing about advertising and would have to hire someone. And what about the video crew? If he sang, they would go berserk right there, and the commercial wouldn't get made.

He became depressed. He started drinking more and eating less. Even the vacuous, accommodating Isabel couldn't cheer him up. She even offered to call up strange girls for him. It was no use.

Regino spent all of his time in his room planning. He didn't bathe or open the windows. The air got rank. Somehow, he would have to pull it off. He would have to equip everyone on the set with gauze and headphones. And when it came time to edit the commercial, the editor would have to be protected. There were other considerations, too. For instance, what about the technicians who programmed the commercial each night for broadcast. Where did it all end?

After weeks of calling and planning, Regino emerged from his room gaunt and lifeless. He had poured his heart into his work. The result was four three-inch binders of notes and six cardboard storage boxes of backup material. He was ready.

"*Mami*, I need seven hundred and fifty thousand dollars. Can you get it for me right away?"

"Of course, Regino. Anything you say."

She pulled out her checkbook, and his eyes sparkled. People who said money wasn't the answer were idiots.

"When's dinner?"

"I don't know, dear."

"Why not?"

"Well, the grocery store has cut us off. And so has the butcher. I meant to tell you, but you were so busy with your work."

"What!"

He grabbed her checkbook and saw all of the checks she had written over the past several months. Grocery, meat market, department store, art gallery. Each amount was entered neatly and the balance updated. But at some point, the balance had dipped below zero and there were no subsequent deposits to bring it back up.

Regino's heart felt thick and painful. All this time, his mother had been buying him things and never admitted that her money—all of the money they had in the world— was gone.

As he flipped frantically through the pages of the check register, the lights dimmed, then went out altogether.

"Well, that's the power company," she said.

"Call someone! Get it back on!"

"The phone's been dead since Tuesday."

"Let me think, just let me think!"

He needed the old Isabel—the conniving one. *She* would know what to do. She would take charge. But he couldn't risk it. He might do irreparable damage, and he would have to explain a dead mommy. Felix would like that just fine.

"Tell me, mother," he said. "Isn't the house paid for?"

"Why, yes."

"And can't we borrow against it to pay off some of these bills?"

"I suppose. But shouldn't someone be working? I mean, the bank normally likes to see at least one employed person."

"*You* could work. You could clean houses or something."

She smiled and patted his cheek. "That doesn't pay very much, Regino. But if you want me to, I will."

"No, you're right. Besides, you're old."

"Yes, I am. And I'm sorry about that, Regino. Shall I kill myself? I will if it'll help. Now, where did I put that meat cleaver?"

"What? No! Just shut up and let me think!"

REGINO'S first day on the job was impossible. Felix treated him like pus and loved every minute of it. But there was no choice—he had to go on somehow. This was survival.

Felix had cosigned with Regino on a thirty-year mortgage at Isabel's insistence. And just to show there were no hard feelings, he gave Regino a job busting tires. But Regino had to sign a contract in the presence of attorneys promising he wouldn't sing, hum, or whistle within five miles of Felix or his family. Hungry and desperate, Regino agreed.

As he pecked at his lunch, Regino dreamed of how one day he would sing loud and strong, and bust Felix's smiling head right open for him. He dreamed of raising the seven hundred and fifty thousand dollars for his commercial and ruling the entire free world.

Lunch. On a tight budget, Isabel did spiritual things with Spam. But Regino just couldn't choke it down.

A Proper Revenge Takes Time

IT MUST'VE HAPPENED WHEN MY HEAD HIT THE BAR. I WAS sure one of my teeth was loose now. Rolling my tongue over and around it, I pushed and prodded it as if it were an unwilling dog. Then, in one sickening, submissive sigh, it shifted. I heard a small sucking noise. Then the salty taste of blood. I could feel the sharp-edged bottom of the crown with the tip of my tongue. The tooth was bad.

I had tried to brace myself with my forearms, but I slipped on a puddle of beer and reeled forward. He was right on me again, too. I had no choice but to fall.

The whole side of my face ached as I drove away, repeatedly checking the rear-view mirror. My lips were purple and swollen. My right eye looked like a raisin surrounded by morbid purple plaster. I don't even remember how I made it out of that dive after I cut him; it all happened so fast.

It was late. I hadn't seen any cars for a long time as I flew up Interstate 15 through Barstow—the opposite direction of where I needed to go. My head hurt worse now, and all I could think about was getting a drink and some sleep. But I had to get out of there—far away—from that sleaze bar I had had the bad luck of walking into. Was that the CHP up ahead?

It was no use. I had to stop. I couldn't even see out of my good eye anymore. Tasting vomit, I slowed the car down to sixty and started looking for a place to hide out until morning. Sleeping in the car was out. What if somebody from that bar was looking for me? My classes! I would have to cancel them. Right now, I needed to find a motel.

Okay, a light.

I veered off the road into a sandy driveway and coasted toward the weak neon red beacon. It read MARIA'S, that was it. The path curved around way off the main highway and led me down toward a two-story house set among cactus and Joshua trees. It was old and quaint, a Midwestern kind of house. One of those places where toothless old ma and pa would invite you in for a piece of pie, where you could set a spell.

I stopped the car and got out. An old black hunting dog with arthritis hobbled toward me, peering through weak eyes and making a faint woofing noise way in the back of his throat like he didn't care one way or the other. I waited to see if he would charge. He just sniffed me, turned, and wandered back to where he had been sleeping.

The house had a porch. On it stood large potted cactuses of all kinds as well as an ancient porch swing. I approached the front door. A sign read ROOMS FOR RENT BY THE WEEK OR MONTH. I could see the light on in the parlor, so I knocked.

Some weird kid answered the door. Only I wasn't sure if he was a child at all. He was short and dark and had long straight black hair that fell into his eyes. He was dressed in a brown robe and was barefoot. I got the feeling he was slow.

"I need a place to sleep," I said.

He left me standing in the foyer. The house looked plain. I could see lamps with chintz shades, classic American furniture, and Oriental carpets. The wallpaper was old and dark.

I had a strong urge to get out, but someone was coming, and my head felt like it was in a vise.

"Close the door, please."

The voice came from somewhere, I couldn't tell where. It sounded French—a woman's voice. I did as I was told and waited. Then, I saw her.

She was young and not very tall, maybe four eleven or five feet. Dressed in a simple yellow kimono. She had long straight black hair like the boy and large dark eyes. Her lips were full. She had the look of an early painting, possibly from the Middle Ages. She smiled.

"I need a room." My voice was louder than I had intended.

"Shh. The other guests," she said. "Come into the parlor." I peered through the stained glass in the front door. "What are you looking at?"

"Some cretin might be following me."

It was starting to get cold. I saw a fireplace. But instead of a warm fire, a huge brass pot with a fern sat in front of it on the hearth.

"What happened to your face?" she said. "Were you in a fight?"

"I need a room. Can I have one or not?"

"The room is already yours. Would you like some coffee?"

"What I'd like is bottle of aspirin and a drink. Ms..."

"You may call me Maria. Take a seat, and I'll have the boy bring you something."

I sat on a red settee. There were white doilies all over the place. She sat in a stiff, heavy wooden chair and, folding her arms, looked right through me. I thought she would send for the boy when suddenly he appeared with a wooden tray, which held three or four bottles and two glasses.

"What would you like to drink?" my hostess said, still staring at me through coal-black eyes.

"Just straight whiskey."

"Whiskey makes men fight. You should try something more soothing. Like wine."

"I'll stick with the whiskey, thanks. Is this going on my bill?"

She nodded to the boy who set the tray down on a cocktail table and prepared the drinks. He gave me a tumbler with a healthy portion of bourbon. I don't think he knew the difference. He handed a delicate crystal glass of dark wine to Maria.

"Well, here's to hospitality," I said. "And, by the way, it wasn't whiskey that started this fight. It was some stupid—"

My blood turned cold. She was staring at the ceiling— Joan of Arc burned at the stake, the veins in her neck swollen like bloated crabgrass. Her back was arched. The temperature in the room dropped. It must've been about forty, but she was sweating. Her breathing was shallow, and her skin seemed to be on fire.

"Hey, what's wrong! Should I call a doctor?"

The boy looked on disinterestedly. Eventually, the seizure subsided. Finally, she relaxed her body and finished the wine greedily. Licking her lips delicately and rubbing her arms, she smiled faintly.

"Forgive me. I have psoriasis. Sometimes it is too much for me."

"You just about gave me a heart attack." I finished my drink and signaled to the boy to get me another. "Have you seen a doctor about it?"

"I am under the Church's care. This is the best they can do. I will take you to your room. Then we'll fix up your face."

I had forgotten my own pain. Now, as I struggled to get up, it came rushing back like a vicious red tide. The boy helped steady me. I felt something rolling around in my mouth and spat it out.

"My tooth," I said. The boy picked it up and handed it back to me.

***

MARIA GAVE me a room overlooking the front yard. I could see my car and the lights of the highway in the distance. As I waited on the bed, she brought a white metal bowl with warm water, some gauze, an unfamiliar salve, and generic aspirin. Pulling up a chair, she proceeded to treat me.

"What is it you do?" she said.

"I teach French at the university."

"A college professor. And you favor out-of-the-way places to drink?"

"It's a guilty pleasure."

"Was it about a girl?"

"What, the fight? No. It was over nothing. Some drunk just decided he didn't like my type and started shoving me."

"Your 'type'? Do men fight so easily?"

"I guess. Look, I'd really rather not talk about it. Ow!"

"Hold still, or I can't clean you up properly. It sounds to me as if it wasn't your fault."

"That's right. I just came in for a drink. The next thing I know, this cretin starts pushing me around."

"That's the second time you've used that word. It's French, I believe. Why didn't you just leave?"

"I wanted to. But then he starts in on my family."

"Does he know your family?"

"No, he— Somehow he knew that my family is French. You know, way back when."

"Perhaps you *look* French to him. What is your family's name?"

"Gui."

"That sounds French to me."

"Anyway, he starts in about me being a lousy garbage-eating frog. You know what I'm talking about. And I've heard this kind of crap before. Not where I teach, of course—"

"But in the places you like to frequent."

"Whatever. And here's the strange part. He mentions some distant relative I never even heard of. Bernard Gui."

"An inquisitor."

"How did you know that?"

"I am rather fond of history. Gui was famous a long time ago."

"Well, he's just a name to me," I said. "I don't know why this genetic experiment was going on about him. Eventually, I'd had enough, and I hit him."

"And then he hit you. I take it he was large."

"At first, everybody just kind of cleared out. I could see the bartender looking around in the back for a baseball bat. Generally, I'm not a fighter. But I learned a long time ago some people don't understand anything else. So now we're really going at it, and there are all these new people cheering us on."

Maybe it was the whiskey, but I wanted to tell it all now. I wanted to show Maria that I didn't start this thing, that it wasn't my fault what happened. It's never my fault. It just sort of finds me.

"You're right about his size," I said. "He probably had a good forty pounds on me. And he was strong as hell. For a while it looked like I'd had it. Especially after my head hit the bar. But something took over. I don't know, I went into automatic, and the rest happened pretty much on its own."

Though she continued to listen, I could tell she was still in a lot of pain. Every once in awhile she would flinch, as if being stroked with a hot poker.

"He was winning, but that wasn't enough. He had to pull a knife. I'm not sure what happened next. All I remember is sliding off the bar and hitting a stool. I could hear the blade ripping the leather right next to my ear. Somebody said, 'Look out!' I must've grabbed his arm and dislodged the knife. We both hit the ground.

"When I got up, the knife was in my hand and he was lying on the floor staring at me. I knew if I waited another second, he'd get up again. So I brought the blade down once across his throat and got up. He grabbed his neck and held it tight, grimacing and kind of yelping. The place got quiet as we all just stood there and watched. Blood was squirting out from between his fingers. Somebody yelled at me to get out of there. So I did."

"What happened to the knife?"

"I left it behind. It's got my fingerprints on it. Cops are probably looking all over the desert for me by now."

"Do you think you killed him?"

"I can't see how he could've made it. His throat was sliced from one end to the other."

She finished cleaning me up and stood painfully. As she opened the door to leave, a hulking figure emerged from the darkness. It was the man from the bar who I killed. He grinned at me and tilted his head back. The gash in his neck smiled as hundreds of squirming maggots dropped to the floor.

I screamed and passed out.

I FOUND myself in the basement, tied to the wooden chair. I looked around frantically for my attacker but only saw Maria standing across the room. She looked pale and remained motionless as if waiting for something. The boy entered and went to her. She was having another attack. I wanted to scream but thought about who would even hear me.

"Why are you doing this?" She didn't seem to notice me. "Hey! Is this some kind of setup? Tell me, dammit!"

"No time," she said and started to fade into the shadows.

As I stared in disbelief, the back wall of the basement became alive with faces. Strange, dark faces from another time. Maria now seemed to be much higher up on a pile of wood. Her hands were bound behind her, and the medieval faces in the crowd leered as flames licked their way up her small, frail body. One man was standing there silent, his arms around three crying children.

"Mama!"

Maria screamed with the mouth of fire itself. "Bernard Gui! I have gotten my revenge! I have killed the last of your family!"

I saw a man step forward from the crowd. He was an official-looking person with a long black robe with white fur sleeves, a monk's haircut, and a trim beard. He watched with the rest of us as Maria's tunic caught fire and engulfed her. Her skin turned bright red, then black. But she seemed to be laughing.

"He was the last! And I have killed him, seven hundred years in the future!"

Now the searing of the fire silenced her, and her body became a single ember swirling delicately upward in the heat. The crowd was jeering, but the man named Bernard Gui had a look of terror in his eyes. I now saw the burning through *his* eyes. I now knew why I had been lured to the house.

As the crowd began to disperse, the images faded until there was only the cold gray wall of the basement. The boy came toward me and gently undid my ropes. I stood shakily and faced the door. The man I had killed was waiting, the bloody knife gleaming in one hand.

He whispered my last name, then he was on me.

Something to Hold

THERE ARE COPS EVERYWHERE, BROOKE REMINDED HERSELF as the intruder tried again to force open the front door. Jeffrey had gone out to pick up the wine he wanted with dinner. Dinner! She hadn't even started. It was dark out. Their house sat at the end of a cul-de-sac in Coto de Caza, and it was dark. She had wanted a streetlight installed, but Jeffrey had never contacted the association, she was sure of it. It was so dark.

What to do? They didn't keep guns in the house. That left the kitchen knives and—

Brooke heard a crash and saw a metal trash can hurtling through the large living room windows, spraying glass everywhere. Not looking back, she raced to the kitchen to see what she could find. Knives, knives... But which one? This!

As she reached for the Henckels 10-inch chef's knife, someone grabbed her from behind and turned her around. She saw him clearly—a man who looked to be in his sixties with salt-and-pepper hair, wearing blue jeans, a black turtleneck sweater, and running shoes. He looked as if he could have come from dinner at Basilic. She remembered the knife and struck, slicing off half his ear. He let go, and, covered in his blood, Brooke scrambled past him toward the narrow door leading to the garage.

As she reached the bottom step, the lunatic grabbed her by her blonde hair. Screaming, she swung the knife crazily behind her, hoping to catch his throat. But with her firmly in his grip now, he easily tore the knife from her hand and threw it aside, where it skittered under Jeffrey's mobile workbench.

Now the intruder was standing in the garage, facing the kitchen and pointing a gun at Brooke's back. He had spun her around and, using the gun, pushed her toward the door. Frantic, she craned her neck, trying to see what she could do.

Quickly scanning the garage, she noticed the pegboard. Jeffrey had just put it up and hadn't yet mounted his tools. Brooke knew she would only get one chance. As her attacker urged her forward, she dug in her heels. Then, in spite of her fear of being shot in the back, she accelerated backward, driving the surprised assailant toward the pegboard.

He grunted hard as he tried stopping her. But her legs were strong, and he was old. With all her strength, she charged at the wall full speed. She felt the man shudder once. His arms suddenly went limp, and, dropping the weapon, he let her go.

Pulling away, Brooke picked up the gun and turned to face her attacker. He stood against the pegboard, looking serene. She was sure one of the naked peg hooks had gone through the base of his skull and was holding him there. How else could she explain it? She could hear him breathing erratically. Every so often, he would tremble as if from an involuntary muscle spasm.

Brooke didn't have her cell phone. She wanted to call 911 but was afraid to leave the man out here. Where was Jeffrey? Gritting her teeth, she felt around his front pockets and extracted his phone. When she pressed the Home button, she saw a photo of a lovely, well-dressed woman who might have been in her early forties. *She looks lost,* Brooke thought.

She was about to call 911 when a hand touched hers. She looked up and saw the man's face. He seemed ancient. His sad eyes gazed at her steadily while he unlocked the phone with his thumbprint and pressed on an app. A video began playing immediately.

Carefully taking the phone from him, Brooke watched. The intruder, looking tired, was seated in what looked like a well-appointed library, dressed exactly the same. He was speaking directly to the camera.

"THIS IS the story of a collector—a tyrant—who was married to a beautiful woman. They never had children, and he treated her as just another of his possessions. His most prized possession was an eighteen-inch vase made by the famous nineteenth-century Venetian glassblower Di Piazza.

"Over the years, many fakes were sold to gullible collectors. Ironically, the only way you would know the glass was authentic was to break it. For, it wouldn't shatter into dangerous shards like ordinary glass but instead would disintegrate into a pile of smooth pebbles you could hold in your hands. No one ever discovered Di Piazza's secret; he took it to the grave.

"All these years, the collector had treasured this vase, convinced of its authenticity. He was a jealous man who was never sure of his wife's love, so he would always test her by being mean to her—nothing physical, though. What he engaged in could be called emotional violence.

"One night, he invited an acquaintance—another collector—for dinner. Over an extravagant meal, they talked about art and life, and the acquaintance noticed immediately how the wife acted in her husband's presence. After dinner, the collector could not resist showing off his treasure. Carefully examining it, the dinner guest declared it a fake.

"The collector was incensed and insisted the vase was real. But his guest confidently stated he knew what he was talking about. He claimed to have lived in Venice for some years, and during that time, he had acquired many rare glass objects. He had even apprenticed with a famous glassblower. He studied every important work there— including everything Di Piazza ever made—and he was certain this vase was a fake.

"'But the only way to actually know,' the collector said, "'is to break the glass.'

"'Then why not do it?'

"'Get out!' the collector said.

"'Why? What are you afraid of?'

"The dinner guest spoke of the power of faith in things authentic. He used love as an example, then mentioned religion. Holding the vase in his arms like a child, the collector became sullen and started drinking.

"After dinner when the guest had left, the collector sat dejectedly in front of his vase. It was then his wife, wearing her coat and carrying a bag, announced she was leaving him forever. She told him he was incapable of true love, and after all these years, he even doubted the vase he was so protective of. Then, with angry tears, she laughed in his face and called him a fool.

152

"In a drunken rage, the collector threw the vase to the floor, where it disintegrated into a pile of sparkling glass pebbles he could easily hold in his hand.

"'I don't understand,' he said, gazing at the destruction. 'That man was a liar—he couldn't even tell a genuine Di Piazza from a fake!'

"'That's because he's not an art collector,' she said. 'He's my friend and knows nothing about Venetian glass. I tricked you into inviting him here tonight. I wanted to make sure you were left with nothing—not even the vase. I wanted you to feel what I've felt for twelve years.'

"'But I love you,' he said.

"Taking one of the pebbles as a souvenir, she left him."

AS THE VIDEO ENDED, Brooke stared at her assailant, who was barely alive now, and put down the phone.

"Why did you tell me that story?" she said. "Are you that man?"

His voice was a harsh whisper punctuated by the stutter of short gasps. "Jeffrey…won't be coming back," he said, barely conscious now.

"What?"

"Because I can't…give him the signal. That it's safe… to return."

The intruder was silent now as Brooke stared at him in dawning horror. They'd been married five years—a long time in Coto de Caza. How could Jeffrey want her dead? Memories flashed across her mind. Their storybook wedding at the Ritz Carlton. The honeymoon in Europe. Jeffrey had planned for them to be away six weeks.

They had started in London, then made their way to the continent. First Paris, then Rome, then Venice. But something happened. Jeffrey had been called back to the states on important business. He never explained why. Something about accounting irregularities just prior to the company's quarterly earnings call. By the time they'd moved into their new home, things at work had sorted themselves out, and Brooke didn't think any more about it.

Though she hadn't wanted to admit it at the time, Jeffrey was different. And it seemed it happened after that phone call while they were staying at the Hotel Excelsior in Venice. During their engagement, Jeffrey had spoken often about wanting a family. But now, whenever Brooke brought up having children, her husband either changed the subject or became sullen. Finally, she stopped asking and contented herself with being the wife of a wealthy businessman. And it seemed to work, although there were times when she was terribly sad and eventually sought help from a therapist. He encouraged her to share her feelings with Jeffrey, but she didn't. Had she been afraid?

Then last month, her father called her, wondering why out of the blue Jeffrey would be contacting him, asking for a loan. She had been shocked to hear it and tried convincing her father she knew nothing about it. Later, when she asked Jeffrey, he told her he had meant to keep that "between the men." He hadn't wanted to worry her. She decided not to pursue it any further.

Now the realization that her husband wanted her dead hit her full on, and Brooke stared at the dying man, her eyes blind with tears of rage.

"Is there an insurance policy? Is that what this is about?"

He stared at her in silence. She wanted to hurt him further to get him to talk. But it was hopeless. Then his phone buzzed. She held it up to her face and wanted to vomit. It was Jeffrey's number. Trembling, she answered it.

"Hello?"

Brooke heard a gasp, then the phone went silent. She turned to the intruder, who smiled at her contentedly and closed his eyes.

He was dead.

As she dialed 911, the garage door opened suddenly, almost causing her to drop the phone. Instead of pulling into the garage, Jeffrey turned off the engine and got out, forgetting to switch off the headlights. Nervously, he stood in front of the car, looking first at the dead man, then at his wife, who was holding the phone in one hand and the gun in the other.

Brooke wanted to say something but couldn't even imagine what words she could possibly use to confront the man she thought she knew—the man she still loved. The voice of the 911 dispatcher came on.

"A man is dead." She gave the address. "I'm okay. Yes, send an ambulance. Yes, he's still here in the garage. I don't know his name. No, I don't think he was high. No, no children. I'm the victim."

As Brooke answered the dispatcher's endless questions, she kept staring at her husband, who made no move to come inside. After a few moments, she disconnected and laid the phone down. But she didn't let go of the gun. She kept it close—very close.

Because, after everything that happened tonight, she needed something to hold.

The Widow and Her Magician

THE DISSONANT BELLS OF THE CHURCH OF SAN IGNACIO
de Loyola would not be rung for Ignacio Muñoz, or
"Ignacio the Mystifier" as he was known to everyone in the
village and had been known to three generations of children whom he delighted with his peasant magic. There
were the shy metallic balls that seemed to appear from
nowhere, float perilously close to pinched, eager faces, then
vanish. Multi-colored scarves extracted from a startled
woman's ear like stolen dreams. Mourning doves that
cooed from the depths of a troubled soul then raced to the
sun from smooth, bare palms that held no secrets. He had
been named after the saint for whom the seventeenth-
century mission church was built. Still, no bells would be
rung for him in these his last hours.

The reticent old man in Roman robes with bursitis who
presided over the ancient, dwindling congregation soberly
recalled the story of how his predecessor, who had
baptized Ignacio, cut his thumb on an invisible sliver of
mirrored glass as he made the Sign of the Cross with
chrism on the child's forehead. Obliged to hear his confes-

sion hours before the magician was to be led to the gallows, Fr. Altmann could not silence the incessant wailing of the women or his throbbing conscience.

"Damn these infernal widows!" the priest said as he tried hopelessly to sleep in his cramped, cold room with a single mothy woolen blanket to keep him warm.

Though he was only sixty, he felt eighty and still boiled when he read Voltaire. His father had been a retired *bier-brauer* who had come to this country and married a local girl. Fr. Altmann detested beer but dutifully drank a toast to his father's good health once a year on his birthday until his uneventful death only two years earlier. The priest had lost his mother two years before that and fully expected that he or someone close would die very soon since he knew the two-year interval had passed and that Death comes in threes.

The voices seemed to come from everywhere and nowhere like the Mystifier's doves. They trilled in the darkness, defying the sun to show its first cowardly rays and mocking it bitterly as blackness carpeted the rugged foothills like a slow, creeping algae. As the wind carried the distraught voices of the demented hags, some of them toothless but their eyes still bright in the harsh yellow light of a fallen moon, Ignacio slept alone on a simple straw mat in a damp cell in a drafty storage room in the church that served as the village's only jail. Despite the inconvenience, he slept deeply, serenaded by the mournful wailing, dreaming of coffee and crickets.

LOURDES NAVARRO DE LEON'S voice grew hoarse as the night turned bitter cold. Everyone still referred to her as the mayor's daughter, though her father had died some twenty years earlier. She had been the first and never forgot the wonder of those rude, searching conjurer's hands that had never known physical labor.

It had been barely ten months since her husband died. She recalled that endless road of sleepless nights, imagining her husband still next to her breathing like the dead. She recalled, too, the stinging loneliness of widowhood gilded with the good intentions of concerned friends and neighbors. All color had been removed from her life. The black clothing Lourdes wore constantly reminded her of the eternal night she shared with the other widows of the wayworn village. She went to Mass every morning and prayed every night. Nothing helped.

After a time, she stopped going to confession because the only thing she had to confess was that she had not sinned. Fr. Altmann had insisted she examine her deepest thoughts and feelings, but the only thing she could think to admit was that her legs were throbbing from so much kneeling.

Coming out of Mass one morning, Lourdes saw Ignacio and smiled as she suddenly remembered that he had been known as "Nacho" when they were children. He was entertaining a baby. The young mother, who couldn't have been more than seventeen, thanked him and gave him a coin as she made her way into the church for a blessing. He thanked her with the humility of an altar boy, then smiled wickedly at Lourdes as he pocketed the cash.

It was the look that did it. Lourdes remembered Ignacio had smiled just that way when they were both nine and alone in the park. Then, he kissed her. She hit him with a rock and ran home, scandalized, tears streaming from her burning cheeks. But now, his smile was crooked and the teeth yellow. Instinctively, she looked for rock, but the scar where she had hit him mocked her, and she laughed at her own foolishness.

Some time later, the laughing became caresses, and the caresses lost hours in the misty sweetness of honeyed nights. He never asked, only gave. Never spoke, only listened. And Lourdes freed herself from herself with the Mystifier as her dark witness.

"I refuse to love you," she said to him.

The other widows of the village learned through intuition what was going on right under their noses, and they were scandalized and fascinated. How they, too, longed for an intimacy that had been denied them for so long. How they wanted strange hands—those dove's hands—to tear away the suffocating blackness and reveal a fire that still burned madly, inextinguishable.

When Lourdes' neighbor Luz Olveida Sanchez found her way to Ignacio's house at the edge of the village, Lourdes said nothing. In truth, she was relieved and thankful that another had joined the lonely pilgrimage. But what started as a trickle became a torrent as more widows availed themselves of that sly sorcerer's charms. Like school girls, women in black would greet each other on the road coming and going, one flushed and sated, the other tingling with anticipation as she carried the food she would later cook for him.

Eventually, things became so complicated that Lourdes was compelled to act as secretary and kept a strict schedule so as to avoid a *bochorno*. She wrote in a plain diary with a sturdy black cover and kept it hidden in a foxhole beneath a shrine to the Blessed Virgin hewn from rock. Passing travelers never imagined their proximity to that chronicle of indulgence as they stopped on the road to offer prayers and beg for intercessions.

Weeks passed, and the pilgrimage went on, even during

the rains. Often, Fr. Altmann would notice these women on the mountain road as he tended the modest graveyard behind the church. He observed them one after another bent in fervent prayer at the shrine, their heads bowed, clutching a black prayer book. The scene filled him with elation.

"God has come into these women's lives again," he said with satisfaction as he lovingly worked the soil in the little flower bed surrounding the sainted former pastor's grave.

The words had barely left his lips when he heard a disturbing thudding noise coming from somewhere in the cemetery. Frightened, he gathered up his gardening tools and hurried away, hoping it was his imagination.

One morning at Mass, Fr. Altmann became inspired, and in one of his rarely eloquent homilies, he spoke of singular women devoting themselves to a life of prayer and self-sacrifice, trudging through wind and rain like postmen, enduring untold hardships to honor the Virgin Mary. Listening to that confused old man, it was all the widows could do not to laugh. They had to hold themselves tightly, and some shivered with guffaws that fought to escape their burning lungs like enraged circus animals.

It started on one side of the church. At first, little gasps of air could be heard, followed by what sounded like someone clearing her throat abruptly. Now more unsettling noises—actual chortles that resembled rabid weasels drowning in syrup. Stuttering, sputtering, and labored sighs of frustration erupted as the priest's words took on a comic relevance he never intended.

Soon, the fever spread to the other side of the church. It was all the poor women could do to keep from wetting themselves. The more the priest spoke of longing and suffering, the more they wanted to scream their sin to the congregation. Fr. Altmann took note of this momentous development and sermonized further, believing with all his heart he was witnessing the Holy Spirit filling these women with flaming devotion and charging them to speak in tongues.

Unfortunately, it was all too much for Luz Olveida Sanchez. She had tried mightily not to laugh. In fact, she had succeeded in calming herself into a state of controlled paralysis. Then, weak and exhausted, her heart pounding, she exhaled loudly, her breath like the sigh of Eurydice as she was dragged back to Hades. Finally, she keeled over into the aisle, pressing her heart, and greeted her dead husband, who was floating in front of her in a milky cloud of fireflies, holding a trowel in one hand and a brick in the other, his familiar overalls stained with mortar. Instantly, the other chastened widows went to her.

Fr. Altmann brushed the mortar dust from the floor, knelt, and said with the utmost reverence, "My children, we have witnessed a miracle today."

An acolyte ran to him with the holy chrism. Taking it, the priest administered Extreme Unction and forgave Luz her sins.

———————

EVERY WIDOW in the village attended the funeral. Lourdes wept uncontrollably, her stinging tears flushing away any of her former joy and reminding her that Luz had shown them all the new path they must follow now. She vowed in that instant never again to see Ignacio. But it was Elvira Altmann Lopez, the coarse, desiccated elder sister of Fr. Altmann, who would lead the widows down a different treacherous road like frightened goats, herding them with a cruel rustic staff from which dangled the head of Ignacio Muñoz.

Elvira was an embittered woman who had never married. She hated the magician—loathed him even. Because when they were children he never so much as looked at her. Because he refused to attend her parties even though she pleaded with her father to make him come. Because all the widows in the village were giving themselves to him while she guarded her virginity like a windy, frigid cave that had never seen the sun—a forgotten grotto which no one had ever asked permission to enter.

The old woman had suffered a debilitating stroke several years earlier, and through sheer force of will made herself walk again, even surprising the high-priced specialist from the capital city, whom she referred to thereafter as "that buffoon." When the widows offered to look after Elvira during her convalescence, she refused their help with that sharp serpent's tongue that had served her all her life.

Only Magda, a poor barefoot girl from a neighboring village, was permitted to attend the old woman. She bathed Elvira, washed and combed her hair, prepared her meals, and cleaned her house. Everyone thought the girl was a mute. Only Elvira and her brother knew the truth— that she had taken a vow of silence after being raped by a drunken relative when she was eleven.

During Luz's funeral Mass, Elvira's mind wandered, and she recalled a day when she had been walking to church. Her left leg trailing almost imperceptibly and her raven's claw of a hand clutching her black rosary, she remembered seeing in the distance one of the widows making her way toward the shrine. She had recognized Luz kneeling and thumbing through a prayer book. For a time, she watched the widow and, as Luz rose slowly and continued on, Elvira shrewdly noticed the widow was no longer carrying the book. So, she decided to investigate.

The shrine was simple and unadorned. Wilting wild-flowers surrounded Mary's feet. Everything seemed in order. Elvira prayed, but couldn't stop thinking about the prayer book. When she was finished, she got to her feet and happened to look at the ground, where she noticed a foxhole—and something inside it. Unable to resist, she reached timidly inside, praying to the angels and saints in heaven that she wouldn't be bitten by some rabid animal.

"And that's when I found the diary wrapped in oilcloth," she said to her brother the priest as they drank chocolate in the dank, drafty study of the church after the burial.

"Where is it now?"

"I had to leave it. Otherwise, those widows would have surely become suspicious."

"Yes, of course," he said. "But I don't understand what it's for."

Elvira rolled her eyes impatiently, secretly cursing God for giving her such a blockhead for a sibling. "It's an accounting of their daily sin, what do you think?"

He blinked but didn't say anything.

"¡Ay!" she said. "They're all giving themselves to the Mystifier!"

Fr. Altmann choked on his biscuit. "Surely not Lourdes!"

"She's the instigator!"

"Dear Lord, the mayor would be spinning in his grave!"

Now the priest could hear the thudding sound again, coming from the cemetery. Thinking he was going mad, he turned to his sister, whose face had gone white.

"What in heaven's name was that?" she said.

Fr. Altmann hurried outside to investigate. A terrible wind had kicked up, and he had to fight his way to the gardener's shed, where he found the groundskeeper sleeping one off. He farted loudly, and the priest cuffed him in the head.

"*¡Imbecile!*"

Together, the two men determined to find the source of that unholy noise as Elvira cowered behind them, her face hidden in her *rebozo*. It was loudest at the grave of the mayor. The groundskeeper, whose head still throbbed, knelt and put his ear to the ground.

"*¡Chinga'o!* It's coming from down there."

The priest smacked the gutter-mouthed groundskeeper's nose with the handle of the shovel and pointed a shaking, bony finger at the grave.

"We'd better dig him up," he said.

When the groundskeeper had completely exposed the top of the simple pine coffin, he used his shovel to pry it open despite the squealing protests of the squirming, oxidized nails. As he raised the lid, he gasped at the sight of the mayor's mummified body lurching painfully, first onto its side, then its stomach, then its other side, then its back. He was about to let go with another oath when Elvira spoke coldly.

"I told you it was Lourdes. The mayor never could control that *sin verguenza*."

Then, as the priest and gardener continued looking on in horror, she limped away woodenly in the rising wind, a dead branch clinging to her shoulder like a skeletal hand.

"BUT WHAT AM I TO DO?" the priest said as his sister made him comfortable in his old chair.

He could smell the arroz con pollo Magda was

preparing in the rustic kitchen and wanted nothing more than to eat, pray, and go to bed.

"That magician has corrupted all the widows of this village including the mayor's daughter. Of course, you'll see to it he's arrested and charged."

"Yes," Fr. Altmann said.

"He'll be tried, found guilty, and run out of town, thank God."

"I suppose."

"We must pray a rosary now and ask the Blessed Virgin for a proper end to this mess. And we must burn that infernal book!"

Immediately, she made the Sign of the Cross and said the Apostle's Creed. He quickly joined in and noted they were doing the Sorrowful Mysteries. As he prayed, the words came out, but what filled his head was the taste of the arroz con pollo that would soon be ready.

SINCE THE VILLAGE didn't have a chief of police, the new mayor had to write to the capital city and ask them to send down a prosecutor. After several weeks, Humberto O'Brien Saenz arrived. He was a young man of no distinction and without a wife. His father was a former prize fighter, who with one deadly punch had killed a man outside a bar, then fled north across the border rather than be tried for murder.

Humberto had spent the better part of his life trying to overcome his family's shame, but he was a mediocre student. He had been forced to spend an extra year in law school, and after taking the bar exam three times with the helpful encouragement of his sainted mother, who was forever seeing angels in teacups, he finally passed when he, at last, took his classmates' advice and paid the three law professors conducting the exam an honorarium of one thousand pesos each. Shortly after, he applied for a position with the prosecutor's office in the capital city.

It was Humberto's good fortune that the man he replaced had died from a fatal attack of the hiccups before he could submit his evidence in a murder trial. Consequently, the judge released the defendant who immediately went to a bar to celebrate, got drunk, killed a man, and was promptly rearrested all in the same day. This was Humberto's first case. The man was found guilty and sentenced to death by hanging.

Upon hearing the main points of this new case, Humberto was uninterested and decided to return home to resume courting the judge's sixteen-year-old niece who was not impressed that he'd been responsible for a man being put to death and who would often urge him to become a prize fighter instead. It was only when Elvira mentioned in passing the death of Luz Olveida Sanchez in the church that Humberto changed his mind.

"This will be the highlight of my career," he said to the photograph of his mother, which he always kept with him.

Gathering his things quickly and drooling over the prospect of finally impressing the judge's niece, Humberto headed back to the capital city to prepare for the eventual trial that would decide Ignacio's fate.

"Do you think we did the right thing?" Fr. Altmann said to his sister after the lawyer had left.

"Of course. Think of the scandal our little village has had to endure. Ignacio Muñoz will be banished forever, and we can get back to normal at last."

"I pray you're right," Fr. Altmann said, even as a purple dread chilled his throbbing bones.

IGNACIO MUÑOZ REFUSED LEGAL COUNSEL, which delighted the new mayor because now he wouldn't have to import an attorney at great expense. While Humberto conducted his interviews and collected written testimony, Ignacio went on delighting children with his usual magic. He missed the widows, especially the food. He had gained weight during those frantic weeks but now looked like Death, Luz's own fate having robbed him of a comfortable life.

Aware that the only evidence being submitted to the judge came from the lawyer, Fr. Altmann wrote a letter in defense of Ignacio. In a rambling epistle, he talked about the simple man who had delighted the children and who in all those years had never once been accused of any crime. He argued that what Ignacio needed was prayer and not punishment. And he begged the judge to show mercy.

The priest remembered with fondness the magic show he had attended shortly after his ordination during which the Mystifier, wearing his Coat of Mirrors, vanished to the gaping astonishment of the crowd, leaving only the coat floating there on the makeshift stage, the pieces of mirror twinkling in the late afternoon sun.

Later, men would swear they had seen Ignacio in this or that brothel in the capital city. Eventually, he returned to the dusty, fallow village hung over and completely broke, his burden recently made lighter by one or two missing teeth.

SOME WEEKS LATER, the verdict arrived. Ignacio Muñoz Treviño was found guilty of the murder of Luz

Olveida Sanchez through bewitchment and deceit. He was further charged with nineteen counts of corrupting a widow. The charge of stealing from the church's poor box was dismissed for lack of evidence. As a result, the magician was to be hanged by the neck until he was dead.

Unable to sleep and aching from head to toe, Fr. Altmann climbed out of bed and pushed open the window.

"It's not my fault!" he said as the wind forced its way into his room, returning to him his own voice and bringing with it stinging dirt, dry leaves, and sharp twigs that tore at his face and arms. Still, the tuneless birdsong of the widows continued.

The old man stood there, weeping. "Dear God, it's not my fault."

HUMBERTO O'BRIEN SAENZ stood grimly in the cold breaking light of dawn as the sentence was read. Farther away behind a barricade manned by two disinterested policemen, Fr. Altmann, Elvira, the widows, and other curious onlookers awaited what could not be stopped.

As the sun rose, Ignacio, his hands bound behind his back, was led up the steps of the newly constructed gallows by another policeman to where the hooded hangman stood, waiting. Though he had refused absolution, Fr. Altmann had given it to him anyway, more to assuage his own guilt at setting this heartless machinery in motion.

Everyone in charge understood that Ignacio had but a single request—to wear his magical Coat of Mirrors. Humberto had objected on the grounds that this was not a street performance but relented when pressed by the supplications of the remorseful priest and the wailing of the sorrowful women.

The bailiff turned and signaled to Lourdes, who had been guarding an old suitcase tied with rope. Moving stiffly around the barrier past a yawning policeman, she felt her heart would stop and wished now that she, too, could die rather than see this injustice carried out. Nevertheless, she formally handed the suitcase to the bailiff, who laid it on the ground, untied the fraying rope, and carefully removed a long black coat glistening with pieces of mirror intermingled with the three hundred religious medals Lourdes and the other widows had sewn on by hand to replace the original silver sequins.

The bailiff marched up the steps, and, as instructed, carefully placed the garment around Ignacio's bony shoulders, then made his way back down to the safety of the earth. Newly refurbished, the coat made an impressive sight. The sun's rays shone over the church and through the trees, and people had to shield their eyes from the white-hot light that reflected back at them.

Lourdes felt weak and nearly passed out as a stiff new rope was placed around Ignacio's neck. She watched as his feet were positioned in the "T" that had been drawn in chalk on the trap door. Then, she steadied herself against Fr. Altmann's shoulder. Ignoring his sister's scowl, he gently patted her hand.

"I refuse to mourn him," Lourdes said.

All around the priest, the other widows wept softly and muttered a steady drone of prayers for the soul of Ignacio Muñoz. It was the sound of bees at work, their chorus producing the honey that would sustain him in his dark journey and, with luck, help him avoid hell on the way to a better eternity.

While the hangman made his way down the steps to

the operating lever that would send the prisoner hurtling into a black pit of Death, Ignacio smiled gently at Lourdes as if to say "Have faith!" For Lourdes, this was hilarious coming from a man who had never embraced God or religion, and she smiled secretly.

Alone and blindingly bright now, the magician stood motionless, waiting for the hangman to remove the safety pin and pull the lever. The only sound now was a gentle wind through the trees that carried the soft voices of the widows.

Without fanfare, the hangman pulled the lever, and the trap door banged open horribly, creating a shudder that washed over the audience like acid. Fr. Altmann had already closed his eyes, unable to face the sight of Ignacio's legs dangling lifelessly under the gallows. But then, he heard Lourdes gasp as the hangman let loose a string of obscenities.

When the priest opened his eyes, he saw the still rope and the Coat of Mirrors gently floating upward into a cloudless sky as if summoned by God for a royal banquet.

Quickly, the incensed hangman ran up the steps and peered into the hole the trap door had left, and Fr. Altmann heard himself laughing with a joy he hadn't felt in years. Without ever having to see for himself, he knew that what the hangman had discovered in the dangling noose was not a body but simply air.

Ignacio the Mystifier had cheated Death.

TRIUMPHANT over the successful prosecution and eventual execution of a murderer even though there was no corpse, Humberto returned to the capital city and paid a visit to the judge's reticent niece only to learn she had sailed away to Paris to study art and music. Not long after, he received the unhappy news that she had become engaged to a magician.

Under the gentle guidance of Lourdes Navarro de Leon, the widows took over the house of Ignacio Muñoz and transformed it into a meeting place where they would pray, knit, drink chocolate, and play cards. In a gesture of goodwill, they invited Elvira and hoped that someday she would accept. It was said that Ignacio would appear to the widows from time to time to perform magic, but none of these women ever spoke of it.

Fr. Altmann retired as pastor and spent his days tending the trees and the flowers in the church cemetery. A young priest from the capital city took over as pastor. He seemed to be filled with the Holy Spirit and referred lovingly to his flock as his children. Elvira Altmann Lopez thought he was tedious and privately called him "that wet-behind-the-ears puppy who'll soon learn what's what."

Fr. Altmann knelt contentedly, working the soil in his death garden vigorously, careful not to harm the writhing earthworms as he pulled up the weeds. Knowing that Death comes in threes, he was convinced that a deal had been struck, with Ignacio taking the spot meant for himself.

And that made him feel young again.

Walker

I stared with blood-rimmed eyes at the policeman. My breathing felt pained and shallow, and despite the gray wool blanket they'd given me, I was shaking. An EMT gave me a penicillin injection while another finished bandaging my hands. I glanced down and noticed the crimson pool seeping through the layers of gauze. It reminded me of one of Lucy's watercolors.

The policeman, whose name I didn't get, touched my arm. "Mr. Walker, where is your wife? Mr. Walker? Can you hear me?"

The words made no sense. Why were they asking me that? Mary Kate was still in the house. Where else would she be? This was all some stupid misunderstanding. Why was I bleeding?

"Mr. Walker," the policeman with no name said again. "We'd like you to go to the hospital now so a doctor can take a look at you."

I felt vague hands slipping around my upper arms and getting me to my feet. I glanced around through blood and gray and saw that I'd been sitting on the curb. Everything in the house was bright. How many times had I told Mary Kate not to leave all the lights on?

A woman's voice addressed me now. I turned anxiously, expecting to see Mary Kate. It was a policewoman. She was young and pretty, and seemed concerned for some reason. What was she so worried about?

"Come on," she said.

I followed her to the ambulance with the assistance of an EMT. I stopped just short of it, because I didn't think I should leave Mary Kate alone in the house. She gets scared. But she wasn't alone. There were all those strangers.

People wearing police uniforms and others in plain-clothes came and went through the open front door. I wanted to tell them to wipe their feet—Mary Kate hates a mess. I'd also need to have a word with Lucy about leaving her bike on the front lawn. Seeing the training wheels, I felt guilty for not teaching her to ride without them. How many times had she begged me?

Then I saw the knife. It was covered in my blood. A plainclothesman picked it up off the lawn with gloved hands and gingerly placed it into a plastic evidence bag.

"Those knives are expensive," I said to the police-woman as she gently guided me toward the ambulance.

"I know," she said.

"JOHN, don't forget Lucy has an early day today," Mary Kate said as she poured my coffee.

"Got it. But I won't be here anyway, right?"

"I'm keeping you in the loop, genius."

I sat at the table, sipping coffee and ignoring my cell phone with the one hundred-plus emails I knew were waiting for me. Instead, I skimmed the *Los Angeles Times*. A child had been kidnapped, presumably by a predator. Two teenage boys had shot and killed another boy for his drugs. Some whack job was sentenced for murdering his wife and cooking her. Welcome to Tuesday.

"You did it again last night, you know," I said.

"I don't remember," Mary Kate said as she refilled my cup. I saw her hand tremble, and I touched it. "Where did you find me?"

"In the kitchen. You were dicing beef."

"And you say I can't cook. I do it with my eyes closed." That was Mary Kate. Always the comedian.

"What's dicing?" Lucy said, looking adorable with her milk moustache.

I took out a Pyrex bowl covered in plastic wrap from the refrigerator and showed Lucy the round roast cut into perfect little cubes.

"Is that blood?" she said. "Yucky."

"It won't be once Mommy turns it into beef stew," Mary Kate said, taking the bowl from me and flicking my nose.

I could tell she was worried. Lately, the sleepwalking had been happening more and more. Though I had a packed schedule, I did something uncharacteristic. "I'll take Lucy to school," I said.

"Yay!"

"Are you sure you have time?" Mary Kate said.

"Absolutely. Those staff meetings never start on time anyway."

"They can't be trusted," Lucy said, frowning. "Can they, Daddy?"

"No, they can't."

"That's why you're President of the Universe!"

"What time's your appointment?" I said to Mary Kate.

"Eleven."

"Call me after. I want to know what Dr. Murtha says." I got up from the table. "Okay, Lucy Goosey, time to get your backpack!"

THE DISTRICT SALES meeting dragged on. I swore that if they gave out one more sales award I was out of there. It was after twelve and I hadn't heard from Mary Kate yet. Then I got a text. *Any way we can have lunch?*

After the meeting broke up, I agreed to meet Mary Kate. Though it was nearly one, there were still plenty of tables. I was already waiting on the patio when Mary Kate walked over. As she approached, I stood and pulled out the chair for her, then gave her a kiss as she sat. I knew it was corny, but my father had taught me years ago about how women like to be treated. So far it was working.

We had been married, what, eight years? Right, because Lucy was six now. Mary Kate was still gorgeous and often made me regret my work schedule. I took in her sandy-colored hair, which she'd let grow out, and her blue-green eyes. I remembered how ecstatic we both were when we discovered that Lucy had her eyes.

"So what did the doctor say?" I said.

Mary Kate picked up a menu and pretended to study it. We'd been here many times—I'm sure she had it memorized. A server came by and poured water for us. "Can I tell you about the specials?" he said.

The server was dressed typically—all black with a two-day growth of beard. He was probably shopping a screenplay.

"Chicken Caesar salad," Mary Kate said, handing him the menu. "And iced tea."

"The Kobe burger," I said. "This water is fine."

"Sure you want beef for lunch?" she said. "We're having beef stew for dinner, remember?"

"Fine, I'll have the chicken Caesar salad."

The server made a show of crossing out my original order and, taking the menus, stomped off to the kitchen. I frowned at Mary Kate. "What?" she said. "I'm looking out for your health."

"Come on, what did she say?"

She toyed with her silverware, refusing to make eye contact. "That it's nothing unusual. I'm probably stressed, that's all."

"Did she prescribe anything?"

"Klonopin. But I don't want to take it."

"Don't tell me, dry mouth."

"Worse. Thoughts of suicide."

"Better stick with yoga," I said. "Hey, what happened?" There were long scratches down both of Mary Kate's arms from elbow to wrist. I hadn't noticed them in the morning. They were dark and scabbing over.

"I don't know," she said, placing her hands in her lap. "It must've happened last night."

"What else did Dr. Murtha say?"

"No, it's stupid."

"What?"

"So how's work?"

"Honey, come on. I'm a professional."

She smiled in spite of herself and gazed at me. I saw fear in her eyes. She leaned toward me so no one else would hear. "That under no circumstances am I to be awakened."

"I don't understand."

"She told me this crazy story about a man from her

village in India. He was a sleepwalker. One night someone woke him as he was wandering down the road."

"So?"

"All she would say is that he was never the same."

"Come on, that's just some superstition."

"No, there were other stories. She said the best thing is to do what you're doing. Don't wake me. Make sure I'm safe and get me back into bed."

"What if I were to wake you in a 'special way'?"

"Under *no circumstances* are you to wake me."

"Fine," I said as the food arrived.

AT MY SUGGESTION, Mary Kate signed up for a yoga class. Things were okay for a while, and we forgot about what had happened. Fall was coming. Work continued to pile up, which was the way I preferred it. Lucy lost another tooth. Then one night, I awoke from a horrible dream.

All I remember was that the moon was very close, incredibly huge through the open windows. Mary Kate was standing at the foot of our bed in her nightgown, screaming silently and reaching for me with outstretched arms. Bloody, gray, animal-like hands emanating from a wet, amorphous, pulsing pestilence were clinging to her slender body and dragging her toward the windows.

I tried getting out of bed, but I couldn't move. The only sound was an insect-like drone that reminded me of a trip I once made to Texas. It was the year of the cicadas, and the noise was maddening. Inside the droning, I heard dark, whispering voices.

I opened my eyes and grabbed my cell phone from the nightstand, the remnants of the dream and the chittering still in my head. It was after three. I turned and found that I was alone.

Not again.

I padded downstairs in pajama bottoms and an under-shirt, expecting to find Mary Kate in the kitchen or the living room or the laundry room—places she had ended up on past nighttime outings. Panicked, I searched the house, starting with Lucy's room. Our daughter was asleep, the spin-shade night-light casting images of the cow jumping over the moon. No Mary Kate.

Next I went into the garage. I had heard stories about people taking the car out in their sleep. Visions of Mary Kate driving the wrong way on the freeway played in my head. When I didn't find her there, I came back and went out the front door, which was unlocked.

Mary Kate was standing in the middle of the road in her nightgown, staring motionless at the moon. *Don't wake her.*

A car turned a corner and, from the sound of the screeching tires, I could tell it was going too fast. As I ran toward Mary Kate, the headlight beams splashed onto her through the filmy fabric of her nightgown, exposing her naked body.

Don't wake her.

A car horn blasted as both the car and I approached Mary Kate at the same time. As the car raced past, I grabbed her, and we tumbled onto a neighbor's lawn. The car sped by, its horn blaring, and hit a garbage can as it rounded another corner. I heard faraway voices laughing and cursing.

"Oh God, that was close," I said. I turned Mary Kate over. Incredibly, she was still asleep. *Thank God.*

"What's going on?"

An elderly woman in a severe hairnet and an old worn

pink housecoat marched toward us, clutching a fireplace poker. It was Mrs. Peterman from across the street. No one in the neighborhood liked her, me included. She was mean, hated kids, and always seemed to be spying on the neighbors.

"Please be quiet," I said.

"Get off my lawn!" She poked Mary Kate with the tool.

"Please!" I said. "Give us a minute!"

"Nobody's having filthy sex on my lawn!"

I turned to Mary Kate and, though it was dark, I could see her eyes flutter. For a second, I thought I saw a red glow around the pupils—probably a reflection. Then it was gone, and she groaned. Her body was suddenly like ice. As I got her into a sitting position, she vomited blood on me.

"What in—" Mrs. Peterman said.

Ignoring the old woman, I threw Mary Kate's limp arms over my neck and helped her to her feet.

"Call 911," I said. "My wife is sick!"

"Get the hell off my lawn!"

A thin band of blood-red rage tightened around my head like a leather shoestring. I ripped the poker from the old hag's bony, arthritic hands and threw it into the bushes. As I carried Mary Kate back across the street to our house, Mrs. Peterman let out a string of alliterative, prison-ready invectives she normally reserved for trick-or-treaters.

I DOZED in the uncomfortable waiting-room chair as dawn broke. The continual parade of announcements and random conversations of doctors, nurses, and patients didn't seem to affect me. I was too tired. Fortunately, I'd been able to drop off a still-sleeping Lucy at my sister's, so

I could stay with Mary Kate while they ran all kinds of tests.

Someone touched my arm. I opened my eyes to find a young doctor standing there. He was maybe Indian or Pakistani.

"Mr. Walker? Your wife is doing fine," he said.

"Can she come home?"

"Yes. A few more minutes."

"What's wrong with her?"

"Nothing serious. She must be suffering from a great deal of stress."

"What about the vomiting? There was blood."

"Her stomach lining is irritated. So, yes, there was some blood. We've given her something for it. She'll be out in a few minutes."

"How long you married?" a voice said next to me after the doctor had gone.

I turned to find a grizzled man in his seventies with one regular eye and a scarred cloudy blue eye. He smelled sour —like he had bathed in a vat of rancid pickle juice. His right hand was hidden under a newspaper. On his left was a wedding ring. His appearance made me wonder what kind of wife let her husband go out in public like that.

"Hope your wife's okay," he said when I didn't answer his question.

"It's fine. She sleepwalks."

The man's good eye bored into me. Slowly, he raised a liver-spotted hand and pointed a bent finger yellowed from years of smoking unfiltered cigarettes. "You didn't wake her, didja?"

"What? No, I— There was a car coming. And there was this neighbor…"

"Shouldn'ta woke her." He rubbed the back of his parched, lined neck and shook his head sadly.

All I wanted was to get Mary Kate and take her home. I hated the old man now and did not want to have this conversation. Then I heard myself ask him why.

"Because there's demons—"

"What? Oh, come on!"

I tried to get up, but the insistent stranger clutched my arm with surprising strength. He leaned in, his fetid store-brand beer breath bathing me in a fog of old-man dread.

"Listen," he said. "They're waitin', see? Out there in the etherose."

"Ether."

"Waitin' for a chance to get back."

"Back where?"

"To our world." The old man glanced sideways and lowered his voice. I thought he was going to confess that he liked exposing himself in public toilets. "You look like an ejucated man. Surprised you don't know this stuff."

"Know what?"

"That when people sleepwalk, their souls are…" His voice became a whisper. "Vunnerable. Like balloons on strings. Most of the time, the strings hold. But sometimes…they break and the soul flies away. And when it does, somethin' evil takes its place."

Though I wanted badly to get away from this freak show, I couldn't help but be fascinated. I had met all kinds in my work—people with different beliefs, most of which fell in the normal spectrum. But once in a while, you ran across the oddball who had gone off the reservation long ago and went around spouting crap like this. I found that in those situations it was best to shut down the conversation.

"How do you know this?"

"'Cause it happened to my wife," the old man said.

"See this eye? First time she went at it with the acetylene torch I kept in the garage."

I shuddered at the image of my own eye being cooked while I slept. "Did she have a history of—"

"Sanest, most kind person alive. Active member of our church. Baked cookies for the kids in our neighborhood. Took in stray dogs and cats…"

He slid the newspaper off his knee, revealing his deformed right hand. It was dried up and scarred like a tree branch in the harsh desert. All but the thumb and index finger were missing. I tried hard not to stare at the stumps.

"That next time she took off three fingers with the bolt cutters 'fore I could wake up. After that, I got the hell out."

I felt sick. My head throbbed, and the room was spinning. It was no longer me asking the questions but something deep in my unconscious. "Where is she now?"

"Pescadero State Hospital."

"Do you ever visit her?"

The old man lowered his eyes. I thought he was going to weep. "Not anymore. The last time was mebbe eight years ago. She tried to dig out my good eye with her thumb. I guess they'll never let her out."

I forced a plastic smile and wobbled to my feet, sore and stiff. I'd have to get to the gym first chance I got. As I turned away, I saw an orderly bringing Mary Kate out in a wheelchair. Her serious expression worried me.

"Hey," I said, stroking her fingers.

Normally that tickled her. This time, she merely looked up. "Something happen?" she said. I couldn't be sure, but I thought I saw a slight smile shimmy across her face.

"It's nothing. I'll bring the car up, so we can go home."

I turned back, expecting to see the old man, but he was gone except for the newspaper. As we left the hospital, I saw a nurse leading the weird old geezer down a corridor, asking him about his smoking.

I HAD ARRANGED to take off a few days, which wasn't easy considering we were getting to the end of the quarter. While Mary Kate rested in bed, I took care of Lucy, helping her with her homework, fixing her meals, and seeing to it that she bathed and brushed her teeth.

"Is Mommy okay?" she said one night at dinner.

"Yes, honey. She's just tired."

Lucy put down her fork, leaned toward me seriously, and whispered, "Last night I dreamed she was in my room."

"Maybe she went in to check on you. That's what mommies do."

"It looked like Mommy, but it wasn't."

Lucy picked up her Tigger cup with both hands and took a swallow of milk. I was about to ask her to explain when I heard a faint groan coming from upstairs.

"Wait here, honey," I said and ran up the stairs.

As I approached our bedroom, I heard what sounded like a cow lowing. My heart racing, I pushed the door open and peered inside.

The room was dark, despite the fact that I'd left a light on. There was a strong odor of sweat mixed with copper, and the air was humid. Mary Kate was standing at the window, naked. Staring motionless at the moon.

"Honey?" I said.

She turned jerkily as if standing on a giant gear that was being cranked. I smiled, expecting her to say something funny or amorous. She smiled strangely. There was something about her face, her manner. She was different—

I couldn't say how. At that moment, fifth grade at St. Monica Catholic School came rushing back to me, and I heard clearly the voice of Mrs. McKittrick reading to us from the book of Revelation. She was explaining that the mark of the beast was invisible, unseen by man but felt nevertheless.

"Mary Kate?"

My wife opened her arms to me languorously and muttered something. Other voices called to me, and I fell into a swoon. She embraced me, making incoherent guttural noises that seemed to come from deep within her being. I felt her hot hands playing up and down my spine. Her fingers were like eels doing unfamiliar things, and I was afraid.

She grabbed my face in her strong hands and kissed me with an animal-like passion. My bones felt as if they would break, the cartilage being torn apart. When I pulled back, her eyes were solid black pools. In them, I saw… demons! Dozens of them, circling in the blackness.

I yelped involuntarily and shoved her away. As I stumbled toward the bed, she fainted.

"MIKE, I don't know what to do. I'm going out of my mind."

I sank into the blood-red leather chair in Dr. Michael Dean's office. It was peaceful there. I wanted to close my eyes and sleep for a week.

"And this is since the incident in the street?"

"Yes. She's not herself; that's all I can say."

"Has she been eating?"

"Not that I've seen. I make her food, but she won't come near it."

"Are you sure it's edible?"

"Dammit, I'm serious, Mike! Grilled cheese sandwiches and soup. Fruit. Coffee. Milk. Juice. She won't touch any of it. Even ice cream."

"Okay, calm down." Mike was in his fifties and had been my doctor for twenty years. I came to him with this, because I didn't feel comfortable going to Mary Kate's physician, Dr. Murtha, whom I'd never met. "Can you get her to come in for an exam?"

"I'll try."

"What about Lucy?"

"She's staying with my sister."

"I'll have the receptionist open up something for you tomorrow."

Driving home, I turned on the local news. A transient in Echo Park had been viciously hacked to pieces. Legs, arms, torso, and entrails hung from the trees like Christmas ornaments. The police were still searching for the head.

I hadn't wanted to leave Mary Kate alone. I'd given her Ambien, hoping she would sleep through the afternoon. When I went up to see her, she was snoring deeply. The sound reminded me of our honeymoon. That was the first time I'd ever heard her snore. I had always found it to be kind of sweet.

I decided to fix spaghetti. That had always been Mary Kate's favorite. I hoped the smell would encourage an appetite. As I chopped garlic, my cell phone rang. It was Lucy.

"Hi, honey."

"Daddy, I miss you." She had that tremolo in her voice, and I knew she was worried.

"Is Aunt Charlotte treating you okay?"

"Yes."

"Just a few more days, sweetie. Till Mommy gets better."

"What's wrong with Mommy?"

"I don't know, but the doctor will make her better."

I promised to read her a story over the phone later and hung up. As I continued with dinner, I saw that the kitchen trash was full, so I tied up the bag and carried it out to the garage.

There were two large gray garbage cans. I flipped the first one open. Full. I opened the second one and was about to drop in the kitchen bag when I noticed something at the bottom of the can. It was multicolored and unfamiliar.

I reached in and picked it up. It was a scarf that reeked of sweat and urine. I dropped it back in and found my hand smeared with…blood?

"What are you doing?"

My heart racing, I pivoted and found Mary Kate standing in the doorway and watching me intently. Her arms were at her sides. There were bags under her eyes, and her face was lined from sleep. Her throat bulged involuntarily. It was like a ball python who had swallowed a rat that was still alive.

"Nothing," I said. "Taking out the trash."

"What's that smell?"

"Spaghetti. I was hoping you would be hungry after your nap."

"Smells like meat."

Her voice was flat and lifeless. As I walked back in, I hid my bloody hand and went directly to the sink to wash. I felt she was watching me the whole time—no, *studying* me.

"Why don't you have a seat while I cook?" I said. "I don't think you can have wine after that medication. I'll pour you some sparkling water."

Her eyes never left me as I got a glass and filled it. I handed it to her, and she drank.

"Feeling better?" I said.

She didn't answer. Instead, she took in the room as if it was all new to her. "Where's Lucy?"

"She's staying with Charlotte, remember?"

"Such a pretty little girl," Mary Kate said. Only it wasn't Mary Kate's voice. It sounded like a lush I had seen once on a street in New York, dressed in Goodwill clothes and shoes, carrying a bent umbrella and dragging one foot that was purple and swollen from diabetes.

"Yes, she is," I said.

It didn't take long to get dinner on the table. "I made you a doctor's appointment for tomorrow," I said, setting out two plates of food.

"Why?"

"It's a follow-up. No big deal."

She toyed with her spaghetti, arranging it in bright red swirls on the gleaming white plate. "What did you think of my work?" she said in that same lush's voice.

"I don't understand."

"He didn't struggle. Much." She sounded disappointed. "Maybe it was because he was old."

My body turned cold. My mouth tasted of metal. I put down my fork and stared at what looked like my wife. She was gazing at something across the room. In profile, I saw her tongue flicking in and out rhythmically to some internal harpy's song. It was black and pointed.

"Does she sleepwalk?"

I almost didn't hear the question over the thudding of my heart. "What? Who?"

"Lucy. I have some friends who would dearly love to meet her."

"I, I don't—"

It happened so fast, I didn't see her leave the chair. In a flash, I was on the floor, and she was slicing at my hands and arms with one of the good knives.

"We want the girl!"

I remember the blackness of her eyes, the breath that smelled of bile and the tearing noises as she cut me. A searing pain shot through my temples, and I saw bright green flashes of light. At first, I thought I'd been shot in the head. A distant voice called out something.

Then she was gone.

Someone was jabbing me. I blinked and found Mrs. Peterman in her pink housecoat leaning over me with her poker.

"You're bleeding," she said. "I called 911 this time."

I tried to get up, but I was still too shaken. "Is Mary Kate here?"

"Is that your wife? I saw her running into the night. I think she's crazy—should be locked up."

Eventually, I struggled into a sitting position. "Thanks for coming, Mrs. Peterman."

"You were screaming like a banshee," she said. "Whole neighborhood's gone to shit." She handed me a glass of tap water.

By the time the paramedics and the police arrived, I was sitting on the curb. The bloody knife Mary Kate had used to attack me lay on the grass behind me. The old woman had neglected to remain. I saw her peering out her front window through the curtains.

"Are you sure you don't want to go to the hospital?" the pretty policewoman said as I staggered away from the ambulance.

"I'll be fine," I said.

I have some friends who would dearly love to meet her.

It was that strange voice coming out of Mary Kate's

mouth that played in my head. A pain shot through my heart as I realized the demon—or whatever it was—had gone to find Lucy!

"What is it?" the policewoman said.

"I need your help!"

I convinced her to call for a patrol car to drive over to Charlotte's house. With difficulty, I called Charlotte and warned her not to open the door to anyone except the police.

"What's going on, John?"

"Whatever you do, Char, do not let Mary Kate or anyone else into the house. I'm coming over now."

"Please tell me what's happening!"

"Just keep Lucy safe."

As I drove, my bandaged hands grasped the steering wheel gingerly. I could still see Mary Kate's oil-black eyes floating in front of me as I drove. By the time I arrived at Charlotte's house, a policeman was walking in.

"Where's Lucy?" I said.

"In her bedroom," Charlotte said. I saw that she'd been crying. She was older than me by two years and had gone through an ugly divorce. Now everything made her cry.

"Has anyone come to the house?"

"No," she said.

Charlotte, the policeman, and I quickly made our way to the bedroom. As we approached, I heard voices.

"Lucy?" I said. "It's Daddy."

"Don't come in!" she said through the door. My blood turned to ice water.

I looked at the policeman. He nodded, stepped forward, and tried the door. It was locked.

"She's not alone," I said.

The policeman stood back and kicked the door open.

We stood frozen in the dim light of the hallway. None of us could move. Charlotte screamed, and I almost vomited.

Mary Kate was sitting on the bed with Lucy in her lap, stroking our child's hair with fingers that were too long, the nails black. Lucy's eyes were wide in mute terror, her body rigid. But it was what she was holding that had stopped us.

It was a severed head—probably from the transient in the park. The hair was bloody and matted, the eyes gawping uselessly. The tongue hung out like a grotesque swollen black worm trying to lick Lucy's leg.

When we moved toward them, Mary Kate raised a gleaming knife to our daughter's throat.

"Daddy, please don't," Lucy said, her eyes huge with fear. "Mommy's mad!"

"Mary Kate, let her go," I said.

"Mary Kate's not here," the demon voice said. "We want the girl."

I watched the policeman draw his gun. It wavered as he pointed it toward Mary Kate. "Put down the knife, ma'am." As he said this, he never broke eye contact.

"Mary Kate, please!" Charlotte said.

"Not Mary Kate!"

"This won't work," I said. "Either way, the officer will shoot you."

"We want the girl."

"You can't have her!"

I was filled with rage now. All I wanted was to tear Lucy from the demon who resembled Mary Kate and hold our trembling daughter in my arms.

Other voices emanated from Mary Kate's body now—agonized, gnawing voices filled with a black eternity of pain and loneliness. What they said sounded like gibberish. But one thing was clear—the things inside Mary Kate were fighting among themselves.

"Put down the knife!" the policeman said.

What used to be Mary Kate stared hatefully at the weapon, then at the frightened policeman. I wondered suddenly whether he had ever shot anyone.

All I could picture now was Lucy's death, either at the hands of this demented creature of Satan or by a stray bullet. I closed my eyes, tears running down my flushed cheeks. When I opened them again, the demon was looking away somewhere. I concentrated on Lucy, forcing her to make eye contact. *Run!* I said with my eyes. *Run, Lucy!*

Lucy squirmed loose as only children can and slid free. The policeman saw his chance and fired twice, hitting Mary Kate in the shoulder and chest. The sound stung my ears. Mary Kate let out a deafening wail that shook the room, and tried to reach for the girl, who was now clutching my body and shivering.

Mary Kate collapsed. She lay there, breathing thickly. The voices we had heard continued in a soft babbling like the internal conversations of a lunatic. Finally, they faded into unconsciousness.

MARY KATE WAS DECLARED insane and sent to Pescadero. I visited her there once, and she attacked me with a gel pen she'd found on the floor of her cell. She barely missed my eye.

I couldn't bear the thought of returning to our home, so I sold it and bought a condo at the beach. Charlotte moved there with Lucy and me.

Now we spend a lot of time by the ocean. Lucy loves playing in the waves and building sandcastles. She never talks about what happened, and neither Charlotte nor I ever bring it up. Strangely, Lucy never asks about her mother.

I mentioned Mary Kate once, and she said, "Real Mommy's in heaven." Some things are better forgotten and buried, I guess.

One cool, crisp Sunday, we decided to pack a picnic lunch and eat on the beach. Charlotte and I read while Lucy played. It was a good day—a day without anxiety or nightmares. That night, as usual, Lucy had her bath after dinner. I read her a story in bed, and she drifted off, her spin-shade night-light casting images of the cow jumping over the moon.

I remember Charlotte was exhausted and had gone to bed around ten. I followed around eleven.

After three, I heard a noise. Immediately, I went to Lucy's room. She was gone! Frantically, I turned on lights all over the condo and searched for her. I found the front door open and, my heart constricting, I went outside.

There she was in her *Supergirl* pajamas, standing in the deserted road and staring motionless at the moon. Both arms were scratched and bleeding.

I nearly called her name. *Don't wake her!*

As I approached, I looked up, and, in that moment, I saw what she saw. Dear God! Demons were circling like buzzards!

Gently, I guided Lucy back into the house and into bed, where she remained still. I fell asleep in her chair and didn't awake till Charlotte gently shook me in the morning. When I saw the empty bed, I got to my feet.

"She's having cereal in the kitchen," Charlotte said. "Everything's fine."

"Char, she sleepwalks," I said.

My sister's face went white. "What are we going to do?"

"I have to protect her," I said. "I lost Mary Kate, but I still have my daughter."

"John, you can't be there her whole life. What if—"

"I will protect her."

That morning after my shower, I got out the razor to shave. Standing in front of the steamed-up mirror, I examined the deep scar that ran from my right eye down to my jawline, where the demon had marked me. I knew that a plastic surgeon could fix it. And I still think about that each time I see that face in the mirror. But I have decided it's better to keep the scar as a reminder of what I have to do —of who I have become.

Every day I gaze at that grim, disfigured face, and I think of Lucy and her future. Every day I pray that the soul God gave her will stay safe in that small, delicate body with the sandy hair and her mother's blue-green eyes. And every day I ask for forgiveness for having failed Mary Kate. There is nothing else in life for me now. Nothing to distract me from my true purpose.

There is only Lucy.

LIKE THE SUPERNATURAL?

Check out Sarah Greene Mysteries and get ready for some late nights.

Sarah Greene has been communicating with ghosts since she was fifteen. Armed with an intrepid spirit, she investigates each new paranormal mystery, even when the underlying supernatural forces threaten to harm her.

AVAILABLE IN PAPERBACK

About the Author

Steven Ramirez is the award-winning author of thriller, supernatural, and horror fiction. A former screenwriter, he's written about zombie plagues and places infested with ghosts and demons. His latest novel is *Faithless*, a thriller. Steven lives in Los Angeles.

AUTHOR WEBSITE
stevenramirez.com

facebook.com/byStevenRamirez

instagram.com/byStevenRamirez

twitter.com/byStevenRamirez

goodreads.com/byStevenRamirez

bookbub.com/authors/steven-ramirez